Explicit Erotic

Sex Stories

Arousing Adult Taboo Sex Stories of

BDSM, Ganging, Anal sex, Threesome,

Dirty Talk, MILFs,

Explicit Rough Sex, Interracial, MMF,

Cuckolding,

Hard Sex Domination, Forbidden Sex

Ivy Starr

Table of Contents

Sex Story 1: Ultimate Confessions

It's just after midnight and I have to quit dawdling; I have to make my tactical move. I'm not a sacred virgin any longer; courtesy to Hugo dealing with that a couple of weeks prior; just before I parted ways with him. No huge loss. He wasn't that extraordinary at being a wonderful boyfriend. In any case, the six-month-long dating time gave me a great deal of experience at sucking cock. Hugo demanded sex the whole time we dated. However, I continued putting him off because I had schemed in my mind precisely how I needed to lose my virginity and it wasn't to him. So I sucked his dick regularly to keep him happy. I eventually understood that it was a poorly conceived notion to wait and that I might be better to have that agonizing first time out with him before I proceeded onward to better things.

The better thing is my stepdad, William. He married my mother when I was ten and my sister, Melissa was fourteen. Mel never truly got used to William, yet I simply adored him from the beginning. He's a couple of years younger than my mother. He never appeared to be threatened marrying into an instant family with a troublesome high school girl. I made a special effort to be pleasant to him to compensate for Mel's uncompromising attitude. I had even begun calling him Dad. Mel considered me a heartless traitor, yet it wasn't like I remembered our father. He'd passed away when I was three. So William and I have had an

extremely close relationship throughout the years. I considered him more as a close friend, one that I've really liked and was my secret crush the past few years, than a stepfather. It intensely satisfied him that I began calling him daddy, so I kept it up.

The reason I'm intending to sexually tempt my stepfather is for my mother. Sounds twisted, I know. However, this is what's going on. I caught my mother secretly talking with Aunt Sasha about her sex life. She said she'd hoped when she married William her concern would leave. However, despite everything, she doesn't care for sex. She truly put forth an attempt in the early years. However, she said now they just engage in sexual relations a few times each month. She was sobbing and said she truly adores him and realizes she will lose him if things don't change significantly. That intense discussion was a while back. But I began thinking then perhaps I could plan something to help. The main issue was that I was seventeen then and I realized my stepdad could never consider engaging in sexual relations with me.

Despite the fact that I'd been dating Hugo for two or three months, I was still severely unpracticed.

So over recent months, I've changed myself from a sweet, innocent, youthful eighteen-year-old girl to a wonderfully provocative, tempting enchantress. Truly, I'm at long last eighteen. I benefited as much as possible from my time with

Hugo, picking up all that I could. What's more, I began dressing more maturely like my mother. Sounds insane, I know. But regardless of her peculiar abhorrence for sex, my mother is a delightful, gorgeous, and sexy lady. She doesn't look forty. She has long, deep, dense blonde hair, a toned body, and dresses to perfection, highlighting her curves. I'm pleased that we look enough alike to be sisters rather than mother/daughter. In recent months, I've even begun playing the obvious seductive flirt with my stepdad. He appeared to be somewhat awkward from the outset, yet of late he's been teasing back a bit.

I decided that I would make my move today. Mother is an enlisted medical attendant and left for her shift at the clinic an hour before. Stepfather is a medical surgeon there, yet he had a medical procedure on his elbow earlier this month, so aside from intensive discussions from time to time, he won't be returning to work for some time. I tiptoe a few doors down to my parents' room. It's not a long way from mine and I heard stepdad attempting to urge Mom into a fast-sexual pleasure before she left for work earlier. She told him she didn't have time and left shortly after. I heard him jacking off. If everything worked out as expected, he wouldn't need to do that any longer. I unobtrusively open the door and sneak in. "Father," I state delicately. He doesn't respond or react.

When I reach the side of the bed, I see him lying there naked. The moon is sufficiently brilliant to delicately illuminate the

6

otherwise dull room. He's on his back with his right arm thrown over his chest and the left one down next to him. His left hand currently sports a lighter cast than he had after the medical procedure. His chest isn't what I would call brawny, yet was to some degree muscular and broad and his abdomen was trim. My eyes follow the dim hair trailing from his flat stomach down to his flaccid erection. It is somewhat curved toward me as if it's calling to me, tempting me, and I oblige. I don't make a sound as I move into bed with him and position myself between his legs.

I lean down and begin licking him, restraining my hands for the present. I trace the entire length of his potent erection a couple of times using my warm tongue and moist lips. Then I suckle the bulbous cock head. My tongue whirls around, ceasing from time to time to inspect his slit over the cock head. "Mmm, you came back." Stepdad's fingers intertwined and lock in my hair, holding my mouth on his pulsating erection, and his hips begin shaking. I continue adjusting my slurping as he grows in my mouth.

I gag as loads after loads of saliva trickle down and lubricate his potent manhood. My heart pounds like a thousand drums on wondering about my stepdad's reaction if he finds out I'm his daughter. I take him deeper till he pokes the back of my throat several times. However, for the most part, I bob up and down in perfect rhythm with his vigorous thrusts. "Fuck that is awesome darling. You've been keeping down on me."

Stepdad moans and his sensual voice strike chords in my heart. This is intensely stimulating; more so than when I went down on Hugo. Stepfather is completely alert now and dominating or attempting to. In any case, I can't surrender the power that I'm relishing. I'll choose when he can come, and I'm having an excellent time so it's unlikely to end too soon.

I begin using my hand at the base of his cock, stroking as one with his thrusts and my mouth. Just when he begins to tense up and stands at the threshold of a mind-blowing orgasm, I sensually tease him with my tongue. Again and again, I bring him just to the edge of delightful climax, just to tease him once more, denying the volcanic discharge I realize he needs to desperately. I had no clue it would feel this awesomely great to have him in my mouth, to finally realize I'm fit for giving him this euphoric delight. "Please darling, you're killing me. Please...I have to come." My stepdad moans. His earnest pleadings send chills down my spine making me shiver and I gag on his pulsating erection slurping on it with utmost enthusiasm. I feel myself moistening in between my legs burning with unbridled lust and raw desire.

All things considered, since he pleaded so sweetly, I suck him with more passionate enthusiasm and remarkable feminine vigor and my hand snakes to his balls, delicately caressing them. My mouth is drained yet I thrust past that, taking him deeper, banging my throat once more, the tip of my nose brushes against

the finely trimmed hair at the base of his potent manhood. I breathe in profoundly, he smells so manly, so staggeringly vigorous. I groan around him and he groans as well. "Fuck! I'm going to blow." He cautions me. Immediately, I pull back and suck once more. Within moments his hot delicious cum fills my mouth. I swallow rapidly and keep sucking, extracting each drop of rich salty deliciousness out of him. "That's the best blow job I've ever had, angel. You were fucking astonishing." My stepdad appreciates unaware of the woman who just allowed him the sensational ecstasy of life.

I rise up and his semi-erect dick pops out of my ravished mouth. "Ummm...You also taste so good, Dad. Thank you! I'm glad you enjoyed it."

"Natalia! What the hell are you doing?" My stepdad stated in sheer shock.

"If you need to ask, then I haven't been doing it right." I tried to downplay the situation. I didn't know how Dad would take this, as achievement or disappointment depends upon the discussion we're going to have, not the passionate and stirring blowjob that I just gave him.

"You know what I mean. Don't act the innocent. I thought you were Angelica." Stepdad gulped hard and countered; still desperately trying to recover from the shock.

"I know Dad. I also realize Mom doesn't care for sex. What's more, since I do like it, I thought I'd help her out." I stated sternly.

"That may be so, Nat, but I'm your Dad. This isn't right." Stepdad seemed apologetic.

"No, you're my stepdad. We're not related, except that you're married to Mom. If it makes you feel exceptionally awkward that I call you Dad when we're together, I'll go back to calling you, William, because I need us to be as one like this regularly," I climb the bed to rest alongside him and delicately stroke my hand all over his chest.

He anxiously gulps and stares at me; however, he doesn't dare to move my hand. "I've never cheated on Angelica, and I don't believe it's a good idea to start cheating now with her little girl. I love her."

I grin at him seductively. "I'm happy you love Mom. I love her too. That's why I'm doing this. I'm making an effort to keep you from leaving her, and I don't plan on letting her discover what we're doing. I simply need all of us to be happy. I realize that lately Mom has been concerned that you may leave her. It's my responsibility now to keep you intensely satisfied so that doesn't happen. Despite the fact that I don't generally consider it to be a responsibility, going down on you just now was my sensational pleasure and yours too I believe."

"I don't have the foggiest idea what to say Nat. I believe I'm still stunned." Stepdad seemed to recover from a sudden daze. I rise up on my elbow and stare down at him. "Don't say anything right now. Take today and tomorrow to think about it. You know I would do nothing to hurt Mom, so I guarantee she'll never know about us. When we're all together, we will be Dad and Natalia, same as always. We've generally been close. However, when you and I are alone and away from prying eyes and ears, we'll be significantly closer. I want you as my lover. Consider it Dad. Should you choose to need an intimate relationship with me, come to my room after Mom leaves for work tomorrow evening. If you don't come to my room, we'll return to normalcy and I won't trouble you again." I lean down and gently brush my moist lips over his parched ones, and head back to my room.

I went out to shop with my best friend Melanie this morning. I got up early so I could be out of the house before Dad was awake. The last thing I wanted was to make him feel awkward. I realized Mom would sleep the rest of the day and I didn't return home until early evening. I needed to give Dad a lot of time to consider what I'd said the last night.

The three of us had supper together. I don't think Mom noticed anything strange. We discussed the start of my college semester within half a month. I told them I had everything except one of the books I required. Mother told us about one of her patients

that had died last night. Father was calmer than expected. If Mom noticed, she didn't say a word.

Mother left for work about an hour prior and I'm lying in bed waiting impatiently. I quit any pretense of wearing robes since I love the feel of the delicate, cool sheets against my naked skin. I continue fantasizing father will come to me anytime now. I need him to see me like this, naked and ready for him. I'm eagerly anxious and energized. An additional twenty minutes pass. Possibly he decided he doesn't need me. I close my eyes and my ears are set on high alert; but I can't hear him. I shudder and look around my room. I must have fallen asleep. The light is on now. I remembered that I'd turned it off before. Father is standing at the foot of my bed gazing down at me. The duvet that was covering me is now tangled at my feet. He is staring down at me with lust-filled eyes and I open my legs a little to give him a better view. "William, you came."

"Dad. I need you to keep calling me Dad. Angelica will get suspicious of what's happening should you unexpectedly begin calling me William. This might be the greatest mistake of my life; however, I can't stop wondering about you. Angelica even offered to engage in sexual relations with me before she left and I told her I was drained. It didn't seem right being with her while fantasizing about you. She appeared so relieved. I decided then that I would come to you today around evening time. It just took me some time to make this last step of coming into your room,

realizing that everything will change drastically after tonight."
He pushes his pajama pants down and his hardening erection
springs out into life. "Do you still crave this Natalia? It's not too
late to change your mind."

I raise a hand up toward him. "I need you." He grasps my hand
and settles over me on the bed. I eagerly meet him halfway when
he leans down to kiss me. His tongue brushes my lower lip and I
open, allowing him to thrust deeply. My tongue intertwines with
his, savoring the feel of him in my mouth. I hold his head to me
as our tongues investigate one another. Father's weight settles
over me and I recline lazily once more into the soft bed as he
ravishes my mouth lustfully. My hips anxiously thrust up toward
him, quietly telling him what I need. For a moment, I feel both
heaven and hell descend into my mind and I feel my perverted
ideas corrupting my existence; my stepfather with me, on my
bed, in my room, I must be daydreaming.

Father's hands meander and wander lecherously and sensually
between our bodies. His fingers ravish my folds. He teases my
throbbing clit with light squeezes, and shoves his finger deep
inside me. "You're so wet for me." He sounds surprised. "You
like my finger inside your tight pussy, Nat?" His lips brush
against mine as he talks.

"I yearn for more, Dad... please...You know that." I reply with
trembling lips as goosebumps course all over my naked skin.

Father pulls back a bit, "I know my girl. I realize what you yearn for so desperately. I'll give it to you. But I need a taste first...only a quick taste." And his warm lips trail down my aroused body; stopping briefly to suckle each hardened nipple before diving further. I sense his hot breath on me seconds before his tongue slips between my luscious pussy lips. I jerk a little as sensational delight ripples through me. Hugo never used his tongue on me, which irritated me while we were dating. I'm happy Dad is the first man to give me this sizzling pleasure stimulating me.

"You taste so incredible, sweetie. This is all I've been thinking about since you left my room yesterday evening." His mouth keeps on working at my throbbing pussy, doing devious things to me, frightful things that make me wild and I feel my heart and stomach doing summersaults in my throat. The delight is ecstasy, heavenly and euphoric. His warm tongue is all over; flicking rapidly over my pulsating clit, slicing between my smooth folds, devouring all the dribbling juices, lastly shoving deeper into me and I shamelessly grind against him like a bitch in heat. My fingers string into his hair and I firmly fix his head to me, riding his tongue with everything I have.

"Oh, daddy!! That's so incredible! Your tongue feels so great in my pussy. Ugh, goodness Dad, I'm coming." I squirm and buck helplessly as Dad devours me completely. Nothing in my life at any point felt this incredibly great. He, at last, pulls back and strokes his throbbing erection a couple of times before adjusting

his hips between my legs. I feel his bulbous cock head teasing me, yet he doesn't thrust right in.

"So, Nat! Are you on the pill, little girl? I can get a condom." Dad asks.

"No condom, I'm on the pill," I respond.

He thrusts further into me and I close my eyes in utmost pleasure relishing the delicious sensation of his invasion into my body.

"Open your eyes. I want you to look at us, Nat." My dad commands sternly. I open my eyes and gaze down as he shoves right in, extending me scrumptiously. I'm delighted at feeling so full. He pulls out and the energized veins in his thick cock are glistening from my juices. Father places my long, lanky legs over his broad shoulders and thrusts into me once more. He's unimaginably deep this time rocking the walls in the profundities of my sacred cavity.

"Your tight little pussy feels great Nat. You like having my huge cock pounding you, isn't that right?" Dad inquires lasciviously. I gulp hard and feel my heart pounding like brass drums.

"Squeeze me you little bitch, work those juicy cunt muscles on Daddy's cock."

I contract my pussy muscles around him as he begins pounding into me vigorously. I can't do anything else. With my legs so high I'm almost folded into halves. I can't lock my legs around his waist and ride him in the manner in which I need. In any case, he enjoys dirty talk, I can give him that.

"Your cock feels so incredible Daddy. I love how it stretches my little pussy. Or should I say your pussy? It's all yours now. You can have it whenever you need. Do you like your new high school pussy Daddy?"

Father groans. "Fuck, I love your tight little teenage pussy, little bitch. It's the best I've ever had." His balls slam against me as he pounds me viciously.

"Superior to Mom's?" I gasp and enjoy the thrilling pounding of my stepfather.

"Fuck...Yes...Far better. Your pussy tastes a lot sweeter than your Mom's. Chews my dick better as well," dad moans and his sexy voice makes my heart skip a beat.

"You fill me up, so great Daddy. You make my pussy feel so insanely great. Fuck my pussy hard Daddy. Fuck me! Fuck meeeee...!"

Father shoves me harder and deeper. His thick erection is ploughing all through my pussy, claiming it, winning it and

making it only his. I feel his hot cum flood my cavity, triggering my own ecstatic orgasm. "I'm coming, Dad!"

"Mmmm, fuck that's it my sweet little princess, cum for daddy." Dad removes my legs from his shoulders and I wrap them around his midsection. He's pounding me slower now as we both descend from our orgasmic zeniths. He at long last begins to soften inside me and pulls out. I feel our combined juices streaming down from my ravaged womanhood. My cum blending in with his is such an intoxicating arousal. I reach down and touch myself as Dad collapses beside me; totally drained. I rub our passion juices around my sensitive folds. Father reaches down, tangling his fingers with mine and we both caress my freshly ravished pussy. "You were astonishing Nat."

"Not bad for an eighteen-year-old girl, huh?" I tease.

He leans down and softly brushes his lips over mine. "Best I've ever had darling. I'm not just saying that. I mean it!"

"So we can do this whenever Mom is away?" I enthusiastically ask.

"I'm counting on it. I don't know if I'll ever get enough of you." I see my stepdad reddening; such a delightful sight to me.

"I realize you'll still fuck Mom, right?" I offer it as a conversation starter. Despite the fact that I began doing this for mother, or so

I let myself believe, some perverted part of me might wanted to have William all to myself.

"Truly, I'll fuck Angelica whenever she requests it. She's still my wife." Dad sounded cautious.

"I know. This is for her. As long as you're happy, you'll stay married to her. However, I need something that's just for me. I don't need you to eat Mom's pussy anymore, just mine. I need to be the only woman you go down on. Maybe it makes me sound jealous or envious, however now that we're lovers I need some part of you that belongs only to me."

"I can do that for you, sweetie." Both of us drive a finger into my smooth flooding pussy and gradually pump them in and out. "I think your sweet little cunt has ruined me for any other person anyway. Angelica doesn't come close. One day you'll get married, however, and I don't think your husband would care to share your pussy with your stepdad."

"Well, I positively wouldn't tell him that he's sharing my pussy with you. Whenever, I want to suck my Daddy's enormous dick, or if I need to feel my Daddy's devilish tongue in my pussy, I'll figure out how to be with you."

"Fuck! If you're trying to make me hard again, sweetie it's working."

I laugh and move my hand from my pussy to his dick. He's getting hard again. I comfortably stroke my hand up and down his growing erection.

"I need you to come and work for me, Nat. Work with me in the hospital." Dad says cockily. We're stroking each other to the point that I'm anticipating round two to begin whenever. I didn't expect him to propose the exciting idea of a job.

"You need me to work at the clinic with you? I'm going to college in a couple of weeks."

"I know darling. I realize you have two or three evenings free every week. I'd like you to learn at the clinic this semester, then next semester you can keep your Tuesdays and Thursdays free to run my Glenwood office."

"You need me as an office director in your new area?" Glenwood is a posh neighborhood. Since the majority of father's patients lived in that area, it seemed lucrative and a good investment to open another office there. "I've done nothing like that."

"That's the reason you'll be trained at the clinic over the next few months. I have exciting plans for us at Glenwood Nat baby. I'm not carrying any of the emergency clinic workers to that area, just you and me. There's a little room adjoining my office. At first, I though it a ridiculous idea. But now, I figure it would be perfect for both of us. With Angelica's timetable changing

constantly we could go a long time without being separated from everyone else here. What do you say Natalia, a luxurious space all our own where you and I cooperate and fuck together?”

“I need that Dad. Let's do it.”

“It's your turn to ride me this time little bitch.” Dad encourages me to settle down on his dick so that I'm straddling him. His right-hand reaches up to maul and fondle my juicy bosom. “Fuck my dick, Nat.” I reach down, adjust his cock head with my slit and settle down onto him. His pubic hair stimulates my clit when I'm completely situated on him. I tenderly rotate my hips, getting intensely stimulated by the sensation on the sensitive stub. “Pound my dick sweet young lady; make us both to feel great. I need to see you stir that gorgeous pink pussy all over my cock until we both come back once more.”

I grasp the headboard and begin riding the dick that fills me up better than I ever could have imagined. Father grabs my waist and pushes my clit down so that with every vigorous stroke it brushes against his coarse hair. Fuck that feels better! I ride him harder. Father's hand grabs my butt cheeks and I feel him raise up, attempting to thrust further into me.

“Daddy, I'm coming. Goodness fuck, I'm coming so hard.” I grind against him, the wellspring of my extreme delight, accepting him as deep as I can and simultaneously rubbing my

clit against him as I spasm around his giant throbbing erection. "Fuckkkk...!"

"That's it, bitch, ride me as you cum."

I think I could be senseless from the euphoric delight of this magnitude. I collapse on him. Father flips me over and begins pounding into me. I was so wrapped up in myself I forgot him. I wrap my legs around him and match his cadence.

"Give it to me Daddy. Give me that enormous cock of yours that I love so much. Pound it into my hungry teenage pussy. That feels so great." My words prod him on and he hammers into me faster. The only sound is our panting breaths and our skin slamming against each other as we fuck hard.

"I need your cum, Dad. Nothing feels better than your enormous dick filling me up with hot cum."

"Fuuckkk..." Dad jerks inside me and he fills me once more. I wasn't lying. Nothing feels better than this.

When father at last pulls out of me, he stands up rather than lying by me this time. "I have to go back to my own room, Nat. I don't have the luxury to sleep in your bed." He cups my cheek delicately and leans forward to brush his lips over mine. "Same time tomorrow evening young lady?"

"Yes, Dad."

Sex Story 2: Collateral Games

It was a lovely evening as Chavez pulled into his carport. The warmth of the late spring was at long last fading away. He'd won his case that day. He was exhausted and needed to relax as much as he could.

"Honey?" Chavez asked, stepping into his home. It appeared his wife, Amelia, wasn't home. Just like that. During the early days of their seven-year marriage, they had fucked like rabbits. Amelia was a lust-filled fireball, with an astonishing body for sure. Eventually, Chavez realized that she was a gold-digger. The sex had decreased considerably, and also a significant part of their private and intimate good times. Domestic quarrels became the norm of their relationship and soon she separated from her husband, except for what she could purchase with her husband's cash. Within months of their separation, Amelia had moved in with another man, Kyle, who already had a teenage daughter from his first marriage.

Chavez went to the bar to freshen up with a bottle of chilled beer. Suddenly, out of nowhere, he heard footsteps in the kitchen. He turned his focus to the sounds of the footsteps. He saw his little princess marching, his stepdaughter, Monica. Monica was staying with Chavez this weekend because of her swimming competitions. A few days back, she had come to see

Chavez with Kyle and Amelia. It was the first time he'd seen her in quite a while. Monica had just turned 18, and she had matured significantly for her age. Kyle was out of town because of work, and although Amelia wasn't staying at Chavez's place, she escorted her daughter to the gymnasium and pools to help her prepare for the competitions.

Monica had her earphones in and Chavez didn't know if she had even noticed him. Fortunately for Chavez, this allowed him the opportunity to observe the tempting and seductive curves of his lively eighteen-year-old stepdaughter. Monica was dressed in her booty shorts, and as she stretched over and around the cupboards for a cup, Chavez could see her abundant ass cheeks spilling out from beneath them. It was an ideal and firm ass.

Her tank top was as revealing: it plunged significantly to exhibit her stunning D-cups, which were, large compared to her mother's because Amelia was only C-cup and didn't have an attractive D-cup bust. The top was likewise very short, flaunting her flat midriff and a navel ring. When she went to Chavez, he could see the exceptional beauty she had transformed into as well, with a pouty pink mouth and saucy eyes. Her blonde hair was trimmed to her shoulders. Instantly, Chavez was hard as hell.

He went to the kitchen too, and as Monica stepped back without noticing her stepfather, he ensured that he could be in her way and well noticeable.

"Oh no," Chavez apologized, as Monica brushed past him. That abundant ass slid across his boner and he strove hard to resist the temptation of grabbing her.

"Oh shit, sorry Chavez. Didn't intend to hit you," Monica quickly apologized, turning her full attention to her stepfather and pulling out her earphones.

"No problem, Monica," Chavez said as he grinned.

"You're home so early?" She said. She was reddening as her lovely cheeks turned a soft pink shade. It looked incredible on her, so ravishing, so elegant.

"Yes. So when did your mom drop you back?" Chavez inquired.

"This afternoon," Monica responded, looking down. "She's...different, isn't she?" She asked anxiously, playing with the wrapper on the juice bottle. She bit her pretty lower lip, her eyes focused on Chavez's responses. His heart skipped a beat; he was finding it increasingly difficult to hold up to his nerves and concentrate on what his stepdaughter was saying.

"What do you mean?" Chavez finally managed to counter, but his voice was shaky. His lips trembled as he felt his heart

pounding like bass drums in his ears and his eyes locked on her hot, little mouth. He swallowed hard.

"Well...she's gotten more absurd. Shit, she's my mother. What am I saying?" Monica turned redder.

"It's alright," Chavez grinned reassuringly.

"Anyway, I'm going to a sleepover with Jessica and her sister. See you later," Monica grinned and left.

Chavez nodded and watched that succulent ass wiggling as she left the house.

Two nights later, Chavez was unable to sleep. He got up and went to the kitchen for some water. It was around 2:00 AM. He was standing by the kitchen island when he heard the backdoor opening. Monica stumbled in, wearing tight black jeans and a very short top. The jeans looked purposefully torn at the hem and were complimented by her strappy, black pumps. Her cheeks were crimson and she looked unbelievably hot. Chavez tried to hide his erection behind the kitchen island.

"Hey there," Chavez grinned mischievously at her.

"Shit," Monica replied, "Any possibility that you aren't ratting me out?"

"Well," Chavez paused momentarily and then proceeded with a devious smile, "That could be arranged."

Monica relaxed considerably, as she shut and bolted the back door. She strolled to where her stepfather was standing to get some water too. She was sweating and panting mildly. Chavez inhaled the smell of alcohol on her breath. He examined her seductive curves while standing behind her as she filled her glass. Her long, lanky legs were marvelous, and his eyes followed the magnificently lush line from her heels, up her toned calves, to the rich backs of her thighs, and the abundant ass barely covered by the tight jeans. She looked like a youthful tempting seductress in the middle of the night.

"Perhaps we could work out an exchange," Chavez proposed.

Monica turned on her feet, "Like?" she inquired. Her bright, expressive eyes wandered down to her stepfather's undeniable lump. She glanced back at him apprehensively. Chavez approached her aggressively, yet cautiously. He pinned her against the refrigerator and gazed at her lasciviously.

"You're a smart young lady, Monica. I think you'll figure it out," He asserted before kissing her. Her luscious full lips tasted like strawberries and cigarettes, and he bit at her lower lip ravenously. She groaned and he tore at the cozy fabric covering her chest. Monica was wearing a lacy black bra, which Chavez unclasped and tossed on the floor. He grabbed her voluptuous tits and thrust his hungry tongue in her warm, moist mouth. He placed his knee between her long, lanky legs to keep her still.

Chavez tugged, squeezed and mauled at her succulent bosoms roughly making her nipples hard and her pale skin turned pink. When they were erect, hard as pebbles, he took her nipples in his mouth and sucked at them, hungrily, voraciously. Chavez began to feel a spot of dampness from Monica's wet pussy rubbing onto his knee. He pushed it between her legs lustfully and sensed her push back, shuddering as she did so.

Chavez grasped is stepdaughter's hand and stuck it in his shorts, allowing her to hold his throbbing erection. He moved her all over his hardened pole a couple of times. Monica kept it up; perhaps, she too was burning with an unquenchable desire for a real man and he restored his hand to ravish her sore breasts. He squeezed her nipples once more when she eased back her hand. Monica felt a chilling wave gushing down her spine, her heart was pounding like a thousand drums as goosebumps coursed all over her lush body. She was working her cozy hands on her stepfather's mammoth erection, and he was more animated with burning lust than he'd been in a long time.

At that point, Chavez pulled away from the refrigerator and brought her down to the floor. He took his shorts off and squatted close to her chest.

"Push those juicy tits together," He ordered. Monica did as her stepfather commanded and he pushed his enormous erection in between them. They were wonderfully soft, magnificently soft

and gulped his whole throbbing erection in between them. Chavez shivered as he felt the softness consuming his entire length. He grabbed oil off the counter and splashed his hardened erection with it. Then, he began to titty-fuck her. The bulbous cock head popped out close to her face. Chavez moaned with heavenly joy and felt his scrotum tightening. He shoved harder and faster in between his stepdaughter's succulent chest mounds a few times more, and stood at the threshold of a mind-blowing orgasm, pointing it at her face. He climaxed in thick squirts, and his rich semen was shooting over Monica's head and tits. She was covered with his fertile sperm. It was an exceptional arousing sight to see Monica laying there in her ripped top and ravished lush body with her heels and pants still on, doused in his cum. Chavez put his shorts back on, gave Monica a kitchen cloth, and left her there.

"I'll claim your pussy soon." He asserted as he left the kitchen.

A few days later, Chavez arrived home early once again. He dropped his briefcase and sat on the living room sofa, unknotting his tie. He saw Monica strolling about into the kitchen, wearing her tennis clothes. She wore excessively short, white tennis skirt, and a small pink tank top. Her belly button ring jingled as she strolled. "Fuck, this girl always makes me so horny," He thought as he called out to her. Monica shivered upon seeing her stepfather; she gulped hard and licked her pouty lips. "What," She responded and strolled into the living

room. She was somewhat damp with sweat, and still quite exhausted.

"Come sit by me," Chavez requested. Monica felt her heart and stomach doing summersault in her throat, she swallowed hard, yet obliged.

"So," Chavez began, "How was your day?" He draped her legs over his as they talked, took off her shoes, and began massaging her feet. Monica hesitated as faint moans escaped from her lips in genuine appreciation and breathless anticipation. He worked his way up his stepdaughter's legs, caressing and massaging her meaty calves. Then, his hand moved to between her knees, crawling up inch by inch. Monica put her hand on her stepfather's hand to stop him.

"What's wrong with you?" She asked apprehensively.

"I am just playing with you. And you're going to allow me since we have an agreement. Right?" Chavez responded sternly. Monica nodded her acknowledgment. His hand continued its movement up to her legs. He moved her panties to the side and began to knead her clit. Her eyes shut; wave after wave of sensual pleasure rippled across her entire lush frame and she groaned delicately. For a moment, she heard her heart pounding in her ears.

"Now, you'll satisfy me. That doesn't mean I won't please you, but you'll have to be my sweet little girl. Understand?" Chavez questioned sternly. Monica nodded and licked her soft lips. He placed her finger at her sacred opening while his thumb excitedly worked at her clit. Monica shuddered and moaned. "This can't really be happening with my stepfather. This is sin." Her inner conscience revolted. "How can this be a sin if it feels so sensational?" A deep perverted part of the mind crushed her revolt. Her back arched off the lounge chair and she was getting intensely stimulated and moaned louder. Her passion juices were coating her stepfather's fingers now, and his hardened erection was agonizingly uncomfortable.

"Not here...please...dad...not here," Monica groaned, still helplessly and breathlessly shivering at the mercy of his finger ravishing her clit. Jolt after jolt of lightning flashed through her spine; she was getting intensely aroused.

"Stand up and remove your panties, baby girl. Then, jump on your knees beside me," Chavez commanded. Monica obliged. He pulled her head down onto his lap. Her bare ass was high up in the air.

"Now, what did we consent to? You spent that night with your friends drinking and partying. Do you think your mom's gonna love that?" Chavez probed forcefully. He could clearly see the hidden tension and nervousness on her face. Monica realized

how messed up she'd been. He put his hand on her reddening cheeks and caressed the skin. A jolt of electricity flashed down her spine and Monica moaned louder.

Monica nodded her approval.

"Say it, little girl. And when you say so, you better say it right." Chavez demanded.

"Indeed, daddy. I am so sorry, daddy," Monica's lips trembled; she was gasping hard and her uneven breath incited Chavez's passionate excitement.

"It's hard to believe, but it's true. Now, I'll need to punish you for your past offense. Behave, and you won't be punished the next time. Understood?" Chavez probed seriously.

"Indeed, daddy. I understand. Punish me as you see fit. I am yours to punish, daddy." Monica panted.

Chavez was desperate to fuck her right then, yet he was thrilled with the idea to punish his stepdaughter and teach her a few things. He lifted his hand up and smacked her round ass hard on her right side. Monica screeched. He then caressed the fleshy ass mound.

"Shh... I realize it stings. You get 14 more, and after that, I am done." Chavez smacked once more, and Monica screamed again. She had the most abundant ass that he had ever laid his hands

upon, and he was delightfully overjoyed to redden her full butt cheeks. Smack after smack crashed on the soft tissues of her ass cheeks transforming her ass to crimson red. When he finished the punishment, Chavez took pride at the sight of the cherry red hand imprint on her ample butt cheeks. He had marked her as his for a lifetime.

"Take off my pants," Chavez commanded. Monica obeyed with trembling hands. She practically felt her fingers chilling down to numbness as she imagined the inevitable. She shivered and goosebumps arose all over her body. He instructed her to take his throbbing dick out.

"Stroke it," Chavez commanded his stepdaughter. Monica took it in her grasp and complied. "Harder," He breathed out. Her hand felt cozy, warm, and mind-boggling. She slid up and down his erection getting her stepfather intensely aroused and agonizingly hard.

"Put it in your mouth," Chavez moaned. Monica kept her hand on the hardened cock and leaned over the bulbous head. She sucked her stepfather's huge manhood and he grasped her hand to demonstrate all her stroking.

"How's that feel? I can't wait to taste all of your delicious cum, daddy." Monica teased.

nugget with his finger and shoved it in. It was such an impeccable minute and wrinkled gap. He twisted, rotated, and shoved his finger to get more in there. She was wriggling with undeniable arousal as he did as such. Each time he needed her to go down further on his enormous manhood, he thrust his finger in vigorously; first one, then two and then three; Monica shuddered with thrilling ecstasy and unspeakable delight. She groaned as if being exorcized and the lust-filled environment seemed so impeccable: passionate moans reverberated across the room. His enormous dick was shoved up deep in her mouth hitting the back of her throat, her ass was high up in the air yearning to be caressed vigorously by her stepfather, and his fingers getting coated with her delicious love juices as it alternated between her juicy pussy and sweet butt-hole.

"You better speed up, little girl," Chavez cautioned Monica. He continued thrusting and bobbing her head down, harder and quicker, yet she sometimes resisted. He heard her gag once, which just stimulated him more.

He was outraged at disobedience and pulled her off his greased up the erection. He pulled off her tank top and bra. He stood up and took his belt off. He bound her hands behind her back and allowed his jeans to follow gravity. He got behind her on the lounge chair and adjusted his pulsating cock at the sacred opening of her womanhood.

"I am going to fuck you hard now, little girl," Chavez asserted. He shoved his pulsating cock in and he heard her agonizing gasps. Monica shivered with unspeakable joy and nervous anticipation when the tip of the bulbous cock penetrated her body.

"Please daddy, I'm still a virgin..." Monica begged.

"Daddy is glad to hear it. You're a decent, young lady." Chavez was, without a doubt, a fortunate man. He wanted every last bit of her, for himself. He began to shove in more as she wriggled. He leaned down so his mouth was at her neck and murmured to her, "Better not get too loud, young lady". He put his fingers that were in her rear end by her mouth and asked her to lick them clean. As Monica tasted her own juices, he pushed them in her mouth and used them to gag her yells as he thrust himself completely inside her virgin pussy. He began moving quicker now and reached his other hand around to stroke her throbbing clit. She groaned at this unspeakable delight; she shivered with thrilling passionate excitement of the highest heaven.

"Oh! Yes daddy, daddy... please," Monica gasped violently but her calls were gagged by the thrusting fingers of her stepfather in her mouth. Chavez put one arm under her to anchor himself as he pummeled deep inside her juicy pussy with bestial and overwhelming lust. Her pussy chewed his cock tightly and her love juices were drenching his dick and thighs. He pounded her

vigorously, roughly with animalistic strength and insatiable lust while Monica craved more and more of the ravishing torment. It was an overwhelming passionate delight that surged through dragging her to the zenith of excitement. She was breathless as she was squeezed between the pounding weight of her stepfather and the sofa.

"My ideal, little slave toy." Chavez wondered as the cozy feeling of the warmth and moisture swallowing his manhood sent him to the clouds of the highest heavens. He had never fucked this hard or vigorously. As Monica orgasmed arching her back and curling her toes, she tightened around his dick and her cheeks gripped around him.

"Oh... no sweet girl, my little baby girl," Chavez gasped, "I didn't give you the permission to cum, did I?" Monica panted vigorously striving hard to calm down her lust-filled excitement.

"Goodness dear. I need to punish you for this," Chavez mocked her. He took his glistening manhood out; it was well coated and lubricated with a blend of blood and passion juices and positioned it at her butt hole.

"Oh no... please daddy, please not there," Monica pleaded desperately.

"I told you earlier, little girl," Chavez murmured in her ear, as he began to twist and rub his throbbing erection around her

puckered little opening with his bulbous cock head, "You realize you deserve this. Don't you?" Chavez demanded as he bit her earlobe.

"I deserve it, daddy. I deserve whatever manner you want to punish me," Monica moaned out loud with thrilling excitement. She couldn't deny the excellent arousal all the teases resulted in her mind and spirit.

Chavez pushed in and Monica hollered. He licked her ear and meandered down to her neck. He lustfully kissed and sucked her neck, biting at it as he thrust it in.

"Shh, quiet now," Chavez said, yet her howls continued escaping from her throat as he pounded her ass hole pushing pounding himself deeper and deeper with every raging thrust. He pushed her face into the cushion and grasped her shoulder. Her screams were muffled; he shoved in and out deeper and harder rippling her bubble butt cheeks. He got inside as far as possible and ravished the tightest hole he had ever had. He began to pick up the pace and attain a perfect rhythm and was completely plunging her into the sofa. His scrotum was slapping against her drenched pussy lips and the passionate moans and sounds of tissue slamming against tissue vigorously echoed throughout the room. He began to feel himself getting closer to the threshold of thrilling passionate excitements as unspeakable delights coursed through his entire body. Monica shivered with a perfect blend of

intense pain and absolute delight as she too geared up for another volcanic orgasmic pleasure. Chavez fingered her pussy and rammed himself into her as far as possible. He bit at her back and dragged himself into her.

He continued thrusting at full strength until he was spouting into her. Chavez had never cum so hard, and he continued pounding slowly when his load was deposited deep inside his daughter's virgin anal cavity. He had claimed her, owned her and finally marked her as his, only his. That was enough to send Monica over the cliffs of excitements and she too orgasmed hard again burning in raw lust and wild desire. Depleted, Chavez collapsed on the lounge chair and appreciated his work. Monica's ass cheeks were still cherry red, and her raw, freshly fucked pink butthole was gradually spilling out his cum.

Chavez made Monica lick his softened penis and scrotum clean. She worked diligently, and Chavez was already scheming to enjoy and ravish her seductive stepdaughter, and how to ensure she stayed with him forever. She was his to be used, and he was determined to use her as he would see fit.

Sex Story 3: Burning Desires

She looked at the mirror and chuckled. The mirror was tall enough for her to see herself completely in it and it reflected the radiance gleaming from her elegant face. She looked mighty gorgeous that day. Was there any good reason not to be? All brides look supremely beautiful on their wedding day. Her dress was as white and shining as alabaster with a hoop skirt that streamed down from her waist, and gradually down to the floor in a bell shape, hiding what she had on underneath. Her top gradually plunged down in a slight curve so that it partially flaunted her captivating cleavage. The sleeves were hung off her shoulders, roses embellishing the little white bands on the sleeves that hung delicately on each shoulder. She was Venus in human form. She looked dazzling.

With the purest white skirt consisting of abundant tulle under it, her train was long and streamed behind with a rose that attached it to her splendid dress. Roses gradually streamed down the train while coordinating with the ones on her sleeves. She looked ravishing. Furthermore, the red rose bouquet that she held matched her dress perfectly. She looked dazzling. Her deep, dense hair was tied in a ponytail with soft curls streaming down and around her face. Her headpiece was decorated with roses, and it was settled between her ears like a crown around her head. She looked like a powerful queen. Her makeup was

brilliantly crafted by a professional makeup artist hired exclusively for this memorable occasion. She just stood before the mirror, her eyes feasting on her own gracefulness, feeling pride for the beauty she was, for the confidence that radiated from her face and the charm that captivated human fantasies. She was smiling, unable to believe how dazzling she looked or perhaps, what she did just a few moments ago on her wedding day.

"Gabriella," said a man's voice trembling, "you look so gorgeous, sweetie."

Gabriella turned around on her heels to see her uncle. Tears were streaming from his eyes as he smiled at her. His eyes shone with pride and happiness at the same time.

Gabriella greeted her uncle Albert with a smile. She couldn't speak. She was holding something in her mouth or that was what Albert thought.

"Let's have a picture of just the two of you," said Albert's wife, Julie.

Gabriella and Albert stood together. Her arm was through her uncle's as if he was going to escort her down the aisle. Both smiled. Albert continued glancing at the elegant bride from the corner of his eye, his gorgeous niece, Gabriella, standing right beside him.

"I can't believe it's your wedding day today. I'm so happy for you," whispered Albert.

"Are you ready?" asked a tall blonde woman entering the room.

"Yes, we are," Gabriella answered and Albert nodded his approval.

"Perfect, let's start the ball rolling!" the lady enthusiastically stated.

The woman was Helena the wedding planner hired by Lawrence Sullivan and Gabriella Belov. Their special day was under her supervision. Lawrence and Gabriella had nothing to worry about whatsoever. Why? Because due to certain reasons, Helena realized Lawrence and Gabriella were going to be a perfect match for each other. Both had very different personalities, but a spark in their feelings had sealed their bonds forever.

Helena, Lawrence's and Gabriella's wedding planner and their best friend, knew from the very beginning that Lawrence would eventually marry Gabriella. She grinned as she looked at the beautiful woman of the hour dressed in an elegant wedding dress, a friend that she regarded as a sister. Lawrence had been more like a younger brother to her after he moved to Russia. She always wanted the best and prayed for the best for them and realized she had done the right thing by pairing them. "Your match is made in heaven," Helena whispered as Gabriella

passed her. Gabriella smiled at her approval. Helena smiled back as she followed the bride to the aisle.

Gabriella and Albert walked towards the door that took them to the entrance into the hallway. Gabriella looked at her uncle. She saw he was holding back tears of unspeakable joy.

The music began and Gabriella's four bridesmaids strolled down the aisle joined by their respective groomsmen. Jane was accompanied by Luke, Lawrence's best friend from way back. They had grown up together. Lawrence was Luke's best the year before when Luke married Christine. Christine had turned out to be great friends with Gabriella and was one of the bridesmaids. She was gorgeous, even with her slightly bulging belly, which was holding their child. She was just four months pregnant. She was accompanied down the aisle by Luke's brother, Johnny. She was in impeccable hands, as indicated by Luke. Christine's sister-in-law, Kelly, was accompanied down the aisle by Lawrence's other friend, Marcus. Pamela, a mutual friend of the Luke and Lawrence, was accompanied by another mutual friend of Christine's, Tony.

The flower girl, Lawrence's six years old cousin, Michelle and the ring bearer, Pamela's five-year-old nephew, Dillon came next.

"They look so charming together," thought Gabriella as she watched them walk up the aisle. Dillon was staring at everybody

and greeting them. Michelle was in deep focus trying to ensure she had enough flowers to spread over the whole length of the aisle.

The music soon transformed from a piece of wonderful processional music to "Here comes the bride."

"It's time sweetie," Albert murmured to Gabriella.

With a smile and a satisfactory look at one another, they started to walk as one down the aisle. Everyone watched as Gabriella stepped up the aisle. Gabriella glanced at her ardent viewers from the corners of her eyes; her heart skipped a beat at the thrill. But her main focus was straight ahead. She needed to see the beloved man and her servant for life standing at the end of the aisle who was soon going to be her cuckold husband. Her grin widened. Lawrence was so tall and handsome in his blue tuxedo.

He stood waiting and grinning. He glanced back at his best man.

"She's so gorgeous," murmured Lawrence to Luke.

"Now you understand what I was saying on my wedding day," answered Luke.

Lawrence wiped tears from his eyes as he turned his gaze back to the dazzling lady that was walking towards him. It was all that he could do to not start crying. He grinned even more the closer

Gabriella and Albert got to the front of the church. Gabriella's heart skipped a beat when she saw Lawrence waiting for her. She was shivering with excitement.

Gabriella was now standing beside her life partner, prospective cuckold husband. Her grin shone brilliantly. Tears were gradually dripping from her eyes as she loaded up with satisfaction. The tears of euphoria were difficult to hold back.

As the pastor said the marriage vows, Lawrence and Gabriella looked passionately into each other's eye. This was the day they had been waiting for. It felt like forever before this day would come, yet it had come at last. They would soon be a couple. When the pastor pronounced them husband and wife, they grinned to one another, realizing that in a few minutes, they'd become husband and wife. Gabriella's lips crashed onto Lawrence's mouth.

Her breasts pressed into his when her lips crashed into his. She kissed him as if she was dying and his lips were her only cure. She kissed him as if he was her most prized possession; exploring his mouth with her tongue and dragging it violently from one side of his lips to another. Lawrence trembled in the excitement of submission. Gabriella burned in the lust of dominance.

And then Gabriella reiterated the marriage vows for Lawrence, new marriage vows...

Lawrence's lips trembled to taste his cream pie, to devour his humiliation, to get married to a bitch in heat. "Lawrence, do you as my cuck husband take your wife's pussy to be your whole world? Do you accept it to be your everything; to serve it only with your servile tongue and lips? To forsake all orgasms and only focus on eating me out after my studs fill me up and cum drips down from your wife's married pussy? Do you vow to be my chaste cuck slave as long as we both live and love?" Gabriella asked that day. And with unquestioning and unconditional acceptance, Lawrence had replied, "YES I DO."

Lawrence was bewildered at what he was witnessing. He couldn't make out the upcoming storm raging inside his life turning his world upside down. This was an absolutely new avatar that he witnessed in his goddess, Gabriella. He knew she had a wild side, but never expected to overwhelm his senses. He stared helplessly into the sky as his mind was conquered by new twisted and perverted fantasies and his dick leaked his excitement.

They walked into the room and let the door shut behind them; at last, they were alone. In a flash they were in each other's arms, kissing passionately. All of a sudden, Gabriella broke the kiss, "Easy now pet. We have a lot of time for that. I'll come back after I change, why not strip for me". With a grin, she strolled to the washroom.

When she returned, her pet Lawrence was naked, becoming flushed as she saw him in the flesh and his mind envisioning their erotic adventures. She was wearing a translucent lace top, her succulent bosoms straining the fabric, and a pair of silken knickers, the material sticking to the luscious mounds of her womanhood. The two of them gazed at each other lasciviously for a minute, Lawrence's cock already throbbing, her lips gradually moistening.

"On the bed, you must assume KARATA for me pet" Gabriella ordered.

He hopped onto the bed, and took the position, bending forward onto his arms, arching his rear end up in the air. His legs widely spread apart; his most intimate parts were left open to her inspection. Goosebumps gushed through his skin. His heart beat rapidly imagining their wild and savage upcoming encounters.

"There's a good pet," Gabriella stated, laying her hand on his head, running it up to his spine, and stopping at the crack of his butts.

"We are going to begin with an assessment. You're offering me your body, and I need to ensure it is worthy of my domination. You do look fit as a fiddle. Good firm and solid butt," Gabriella continued as she squeezed his ass cheeks in her grasp, before putting her fingertips between the firm globes.

"What a cute ass you have, pet," Gabriella teased, tracing a finger around the edge of the crinkled gap, making him groan delicately. His breathing accelerated; her hands trembled with excitement. She ran the finger down over his perineum, detecting how sensitive both it and his anal cavity were to her touch.

She took his scrotum in her grasp, crushing delicately, moving his gonads between her thumb and finger, extending the sac down.

"All appears to be exceptionally sound, my pet," Gabriella said to Lawrence, as her hand continued with its descending adventure, fingertips running down the underside of his already hardened cock. She could feel her moisture in between her legs. Goosebumps coursed through her radiant skin.

She grinned wickedly; she was pleased that this youthful pet's relentless excitement was absolutely due to her presence, her touch, her exotic voice. Wrapping her hand over his throbbing pole, she expertly started to jerk off him, leaving him completely erect within moments.

"Mmm... you are a cute sized pet; your Queen is exceptionally satisfied." Gabriella chuckled.

"Thank you, my queen" the pet answered, reddening at the appreciation, and his exposure.

"Later you'll demonstrate to me how tight your body gets as you cum," Gabriella teased as she continued to slowly stroke his hard erection, "however you can't cum right now, pet. You need to earn your reward by being a sweet young man for your Queen and satisfying your Queen. So, my pet, do you want to please your Queen?" Gabriella teased.

"Yes, my Queen," Lawrence breathed, "I live to serve and satisfy you."

"Good boy, such a lovely pet," Gabriella praised Lawrence, gradually masturbating him until she could hear his breathing become heavier and little moans of joy could be heard, before suddenly ceasing her erotic ministrations, leaving his erection hanging agonizingly hard between his spread thighs, the tip gleaming with pre-cum. Rising from the bed and strolling to the dresser, Gabriella talked back over her shoulder: "Reach behind yourself for me, my dearest, and spread that delightful ass cheeks of yours nice and wide. I want to see your gap open for me."

On the dresser, she opened a cabinet of her favorite lube, liberally covering two fingers with it. Going back to her pet, she saw with a grin that Lawrence had done as she instructed him to do, his hands pulling his ass cheeks apart. That resulted in the crinkled pink opening between them opened wide for her inspection.

Coming back to the bed, she knelt behind him, appreciating and cherishing him for a second. Smiling to herself devilishly, she leaned down and kissed him between his spread cheeks, her tongue snaking out to press past the rim of his butt.

"Oh, my Queen!" Lawrence screamed in pleasure.

Laughing, she ran her tongue up his perineum and over his puckered little star.

"Like that, my slave? If you are good and please me, you can have more like these as your treat later." Gabriella teased.

He tried to reply yet moaned deeply as her lubed fingertips discovered his anal cavity. Smearing lube against the outside of his gaping cavity, she thrust one finger inside, gradually sliding it in to the knuckle. Pulling it back, she squeezed and thrust two fingers against his puckered hole this time and grinned down at him. She was immensely satisfied when his hole effectively sucked in both her fingers inside.

"What a good pet, so tight and warm," Gabriella murmured, "However, I think we'll have to stretch you out before you're fit to be used appropriately."

She gradually shoved her fingers all the way into him for a few minutes, twisting them as she did, rubbing his prostate, getting intensely stimulated by doing this to him, and shaking in passionate excitement seeing his nicely extended rim. Then she

pulled her fingers out, making him whine a bit in dissatisfaction, his anal cavity closing down tightly feeling the frustrating void.

"Right! Where is it. Ah! This one would be perfect," Gabriella announced, pulling a medium sized butt plug from her pack. Turning back to Lawrence she instructed, "Keep those buttocks nicely and widely spread for me darling, I need your anal hole open for this."

Kneeling behind him once again, she shivered slightly as she set the tip of the plug against him. Goosebumps coursed through his skin. Lawrence licked his parched lips. He gulped hard. His mouth gaped wide as his anal cavity felt the excitement of the alien intrusion in his anal region. Squeezing delicately yet firmly, the tip slid into him, his tight gap stretching around it. Gabriella reached around him and stroked his stiffened cock delicately, offering encouragement. He snorted as she squeezed the plug firmly into his favorite hole. It was heaven. She was taking care of her slave, her pet, Lawrence.

"Good boy! Relax. Press back against me. That's my boy!" Gabriella cooed as the butt-plug's widest point slipped past his sphincter and he squeezed around it hard, with just the flared end left out.

"Now, we'll leave that there for a while. I need to warm you up some more, externally," Gabriella chuckled wickedly. "Put your arms beneath your head again and raise your ass up."

As he followed her commands, word by word, she kept on talking to him.

"You must learn to enjoy your punishment. That's a crucial part of your training, slave. Your rear isn't only for fucking; it will also be for spanking and flogging when I'm disappointed with you. Punishment for my pet in my house is a bare bottom spanking, with either hand, flogger, or cane, equal amounts on each butt cheek. More serious offenses will result in a double spanking on the base or the standard twenty hits between the legs. Understood?" Gabriella teased. Lawrence shivered in passionate excitement.

"Yes, my Queen," the pet swallowed hard.

"Great," Gabriella answered, grabbing the small leather whip that she pulled out from her cabinet, "Now, as you've really been a very excellent pet, and this is your training, you'll just have to take ten for now. You'll count each one before accepting the next one."

With that, she mightily swung her arm and the whip painfully landed on his firm ass, making him rock forward in shock. In spite of that, he still obediently counted the agonizing blow.

"One, my Queen," he gasped.

Smack! The whip smashed into his right ass cheek. It hurt. "Two, my Queen!"

Smack! The burn was starting on his left ass cheek. "Three, my Queen!"

Smack! Lighting struck again; Gabriella was impeccably alternating between his ass cheeks. "Four, my Queen!"

Smack! The thunder of the blow was echoing in the room. So embarrassing. "Five, my Queen!"

Smack! The heat was rising. "Six, my Queen!"

Smack! Another flash of pain struck Lawrence. Gabriella was a real sadist. "Seven, my Queen!"

Smack! Like an electric shock, only bigger. Lawrence was leaking. "Eight, my Queen!"

Smack! Gabriella took pride in her ass-reddening caliber. "Nine, my Queen!"

Ten later, his ass cheeks were a satisfying shade of red, the crimson hue broken uniquely by the black handle of the butt plug peeking out from between his two-round buttocks...

"I think we're ready now, my pet," Gabriella announced, smiling deviously as she reached out, took the butt plug firmly in her grasp, and all of a sudden, pulled it out of him in with one tug. Lawrence screamed out as his butt suddenly stretched wide, and she was delighted to see as she inched closer; that his anal cavity

didn't clench entirely but was gaping wide welcoming her presence. He was ready for her.

She opened her cabinet again and took out a blindfold she had purchased specifically for his special and erotic occasion. She moved to sit alongside his head, her lace-covered groin inches away from his face. He groaned softly, he could smell her excitement, he could sense her moistening at his plight. Lawrence sensed how the delicate fabric followed the mounds of her luscious pussy lips.

As Gabriella slipped the blindfold on, she whispered in Lawrence's ear, "The sensations will be electric, my pet. Additionally, you haven't yet earned the reward and right to gaze upon my fully naked body tonight. You'll have to earn that every night. Okay?"

Encased in darkness, Lawrence had his ears on high alert, hearing just the delicate murmur of ribbon and she slid her knickers off. Goosebumps coursed through his skin and his heart pumped faster because he was so desperate to witness the Holy Grail between her legs, to worship her luscious womanhood! He heard her rummaging in her cabinet, looking for what he sensed would be her strap-on. Lawrence pondered quietly how huge it would be. He just hoped he would be able to take her, thereby pleasing her. The pet felt the bed move as his

Queen moved up behind him; all of a sudden, he was mindful of how naked and vulnerable his private parts were.

Gripping one of his ass cheeks in each of her hands, Gabriella spread Lawrence open, moving forward so the very tip of the strap-on leaned against his puckered opening, making him groan in anticipation. Gabriella shivered in the fire of dominance; Lawrence shivered in the lust of submission.

"Is this what you want for tonight, my dearest? For your Queen to slide her huge dildo strap-on into your smooth, tight little hole? To use that greedy little gap for my pleasure?" Gabriella teased.

Lawrence pleaded, wanting her in absolute desperation, "Indeed, please my Queen, take me, fill my asshole, I beg you to fuck me, my Queen." Lawrence gulped hard.

"Such a good pet," Gabriella murmured as she pushed forward firmly yet slowly with her hips, looking eagerly as the tip of the dildo strap-on stretched his young butt hole, the rim growing as she thrust further into him.

Watching with intense pleasure as the smooth rim of his rear-end stretched out as she pulled back the length of the cock, grasping firmly around the pole, Gabriella started to expertly utilize the full length of her cock to open up his tight youthful rectum. Skillfully using her hips, she shoved somewhere deep

inside his butt hole, penetrating her pet with every last inch of the pole.

"Oh! My God, you're so tight," Gabriella drawled as she drove into him ever deeper, his butt hole gripping the pole tightly, making it press hard against her clit.

In a couple of moments, Gabriella felt her climax approaching; she had intended to be slow and delicate initially, yet Lawrence was so tight, and his opening looked so impeccably stretched around her pole, that she really wanted to fuck him hard. For a minute the only sounds were his cries each time she thrust completely into him, the head of her dildo hitting his prostate, and the smack of her paunch and thighs slapping against his body. His throbbing cock and balls swung forward and backward as she fucked him hard, fucked him ruthlessly for her pleasure, pre-cum overflowing from the tip of his erection. As she felt that electric tingle developing between her legs, she forced his butt cheeks as far stretched out as she could, not having any desire to waste even a small inch of the dildo, needing him to feel absolutely full. With a cry, she pushed somewhere deep down into him one final time, cumming hard, gripping his hips and pulling his body back to meet the attacking shaft; impaling his delicate youthful structure.

Breathing vigorously, Gabriella lay forward, settling upon Lawrence's back, strap-on buried as far as possible inside his hot bowels.

"Oh, my dearest, you were so great, absolutely superb," Gabriella praised Lawrence as she recovered, and her lips came crashing onto his naked back.

Lawrence was breathing just as hard as his Queen and could only mumble platitudes to her, basking in the warm gleam of having satisfied and delighted her, having united with her.

After a couple of seconds, Gabriella kissed his neck, around to his ear, and murmured, "On your back now, my dearest".

Grabbing his hips to keep him still, she gradually began to pull herself back from him, until at last the head of the strap-on showed up from between his anal cavity, his marginally red butt hole glistening with lube between them, open as if pleading for more. He moaned in dissatisfaction, realizing that his thirst would have to be quenched some other time. Lawrence was disappointed at the feeling that he was no longer coupled with his Queen and that she was not inside him, making him feel emptier than ever before.

As Lawrence turned to lie on his back, Gabriella removed Lawrence's blindfold, then took the hem of her top in her grasp,

and lifted it off over her head, exhibiting her bosoms to him. Finally, he had earned his reward to gaze at his naked seduction.

"Wow!" was everything Lawrence could muster, spellbound by the vision of magnificence before him. Gabriella was now totally naked, but more gorgeous than ever before glistening in her sweat, igniting the passion in his eyes, just the thick shaft protruding from between her thighs shrouded her vulva from him.

"My Queen, you look so evergreen," Lawrence mumbled. She looked between his very own thighs, to his long hard erection, throbbing and leaking, and realized that he meant every word.

Silently she moved back towards him. As she knelt between his legs, he pulled his legs upward, reaching his chest, giving her easy access to his puckered opening. She peered down into his eyes, caressing his cheek with one hand while she placed the tip of the strap-on on against his butt.

"You realize you belong to me, don't you, my pet?" Gabriella teased Lawrence.

He could just nod his approval, unable to turn away from her peering eyes. Gradually, she sank down onto him, the pole of her strap-on sliding effectively into his well-used rear, until her belly squeezed against his, his hard cock squeezed between them, her succulent bosoms against his bare chest. She lay still for a

minute, as they kissed passionately, tongues finding one another, and he wrapped his legs firmly around her back.

Gently, affectionately, she started to move her hips back and forth shoving the strap-on in and out of her pet's lubricated butt hole, making love to him. He screamed with euphoric delight as her cock curved into him, filling his bowel. Pulling her hard against him, he murmured in her ear, "Cum in me my Queen, my Goddess. Cum in my opening. Fill me, mark me as yours. I love you. I love you."

Grinning down at her wonderful and excellent pet, she lifted a bosom to his mouth, moaning with delight as he sucked on her nipple, the snugness of his body already making the dildo press pleasurably against her clit. Her ideal pet would be very much used for her pleasure before the morning and she was certain about that, and she would be intensely and immensely fulfilled. Gabriella shut her eyes, wondering how she would get him to go down on her with his magnificent tongue in an hour or so later. He would need plenty of time to recover from the intensity of her thrusts. This would surely be a wedding night to remember for life...a night to live for a lifetime...

Sex Story 4: Concealed Games – Part 1

"Hun, can I ask you a question and would you be absolutely honest with me?"

It sounded innocent enough. However, anyone would need to know Priya thoroughly to realize that she had something on her mind. Her husband, Navin stated, "Sure darling, I'll try to answer as best as I can. What is it that's troubling you?" Navin knew his wife Priya like the lines of his palm. And with that remarkable question, she had already stirred up Navin's feelings.

"Would you mind if I go on a date with another man?" Priya asked tilting her head, a serious look on her face. For a moment, Navin felt his heart beating like drums in the middle of the night in his bedroom. "Are you serious? Come on Priya, I know how much you love to play a prank." Navin gulped, licked his parched lips, thought to speak out his mind, but couldn't.

"Oh, my God! Has she cracked my Windows user ID and password on my computer? She must have seen my porn sites." Navin was stunned, yet he kept calm and assumed that Priya had definitely discovered his addiction to interracial porn. He

played it safe and kept his cool. "Why are you asking me this?" Navin asked.

Priya expounded about how one of her friends Becky, shared her sexual relationship with her husband. Revealing to him that Greg, Becky's husband, asked her to find a boyfriend to engage in sexual relations with and that he needed to watch while they were doing it. He truly needed to be with her after she had been with her lover, Becky had told her.

Navin looked at Priya and she simply gazed at him with those bright and beautiful eyes, and anxiously and impatiently waiting for his response.

Without delay, Navin stated, "Greg has never said a word to me about that. But if you're asking whether most men are aroused to think about their wives and girlfriends doing that, then yes, I'd have to agree."

"So it turns you on to imagine me with another man?" Priya's inquiry was accompanied with a dead serious look.

"Absolutely," Navin replied.

She just stared at him after her husband's unexpected reply, Priya's eyes got watery and she began to cry. "You don't love me anymore, do you?" she was heartbroken.

Navin asserted, "I do love you; without any doubts and beyond any limits. I love you. Adore you. Admire you so much. I would always want you to be happy, no matter the cost. If I didn't care about you, it wouldn't get me excited. But I would also want you to be by my side, now and always. I would never want to lose you. Most men are wired to be stimulated when their woman is lusted, wanted and desired by another.

However, a few men won't let it happen or would never disclose their deep perverted feelings because of their macho appearance. Or perhaps, they think that if they express their dark feelings, they would be less of a man. But, believe me, a man who knows a woman is only meant to be in the kitchen, never knows what to do with his woman in the bedroom. Therefore, if their bond with their woman is strong enough and if they are half the man they claim to be, then they would never be jealous to find another man with their woman. Instead, they would be flattered and feel proud that his woman was so alluring that she was desired by another man."

Priya promptly responded, "I'd divorce you the following day if I found you with another woman. I am never going to accept another woman in your life. You're mine and mine only."

"With my entire heart and soul babe," Navin replied with trembling lips. His fingers felt so cold and his heart was pounding so fast.

"I just don't understand men." Priya stated.

Navin grasped her hand and kissed it passionately and then delicately kissed her lips to express his love. Yes, he would go to any extent to make her happy because he loved her so much. Then she was on him. Navin felt as if she'd deliberately collapsed her soft, seductive, hot body craving for something onto his own yearning body. She pulled his arms above his head with her hands, holding him as her willing hostage. Then she flicked her long, lanky fingers on his lips, tempting him more. For a long moment, they were eye locked seeing each other's reflections. Her breasts pressed down onto his nipples, goading them, yet offering no liberty, and then her lips came crashing down onto his. She kissed him as if she was dying and his lips were her only cure. She kissed him as if he was her most prized possession; exploring his mouth with her tongue and dragging it violently from one side of his lips to another. Navin trembled in the excitement of submission. Priya burned in the lust of dominance.

When they broke the kiss, Navin kissed her neck and slipped his hand up her back under her gown, then further down under her gown exploring and over her panties, delicately massaging her butt and playing with the soft fabric of her panties.

Priya returned the favor as she kissed his neck and snaked her hand over his hardening cock.

"So what are you thinking, Navin? You're so hard." Priya breathed into Navin's ears.

"I love you so much Priya and would do anything to make you happy," was Navin's honest reply.

"Make love to me then hon. Make me happy. Show me how much you love me," Priya was burning in wild lust.

The psychological image of his married Indian wife, so beautiful, evergreen and seductively tempting in the arms of another man sawing his cock in and out of her body making her cum again and again, her passionate moaning and screaming out for him to cum in her, was intensely stimulating for Navin. He was passionately excited beyond any limits resulting in the hardening of his 4-and-a-half-inch little Indian prick. He was fast to spread her legs and thrust himself into Priya releasing his stimulating zest within Priya in just two minutes.

Priya said, "Wow that was so fast" and instructed him to remain in her and allow her to relish the excitement for a few moments more. She revealed to him that she now realized men are strange and said Becky was thinking about going out with a guy from her work. She further disclosed that the guy was reputed to be a stud as he had been with a few girls in the office.

"Does Greg want her to be in a one-night stand or him as her regular lover?" Navin was again burning with excitement.

Priya clarified, "Becky came over for some coffee today and we were doing our regular chit chatting when she spilled the beans. They have discussed this at length over the last few years and are now serious that she take the next step and have a real lover. She also wanted to know whether you've ever said anything to me about the subject. I told her, 'no', and that you're not as naughty as Greg is, until today, anyway."

Priya kissed Navin so deeply, so passionately that for a moment, Navin forgot whose air he was breathing in.

"Becky said that she's researched a lot about the subject on the web and there are tons of websites that discuss the subject extensively. There are even sites where you can post your encounters. She gave me a couple of sites to explore.

God, I now understand why you always asked me to wear my backless dresses whenever I went to a party. You naughty boy, you were so horny whenever you found my colleagues flirting with me, weren't you?" Priya asked seductively.

In the heat of the current discussion and the wild temptation conquering his senses, Navin could only nod in acknowledgement.

Navin's average erection was throbbing again in his wife's carnal pleasure hole within seconds and it was rock solid. Priya sensing the urge in him and yearning to fulfill her unquenchable wild

lust started to thump from beneath and soon they were enjoying another ecstatic pleasure ride of their carnal adventure.

"Becky was right; you do like the idea of me with another man". Priya said jokingly, "Fuck me Navin, and don't cum too fast again or I'll need to find a stud to satisfy me."

Fortunately, having just cum, Navin did last around five minutes and truly tried to pummel his wife. Although Priya had a climax like he hadn't found in years, her expressions had a fine line of difference between intense dissatisfaction and tremendous satisfaction. When Navin took out his limp dick, Priya rolled over and went to sleep.

Her reactions made his heart pound like bass drums. It's always hard to transform fantasies into reality. And everything has a price. For a moment, Navin just thought to keep her with him the way she was, and the next moment, his mind was again crowded with tempting images of other men, black, white, Hispanic alike, ramming their huge cocks in her, showing her what a gorgeous slut she was.

Navin and Priya had been married for two years. They had been introduced by their parents in a typical Indian marriage reception party. Before that, Navin never knew that Priya was studying at Los Angeles Valley College in Applied Accounting. She also got a scholarship to pursue her studies in a foreign college. It was the same college in which Navin was studying in

Applied Electronics. Navin had gazed in amazement at the ravishingly gorgeous young lady standing before him at the party. She had long curly black   hair that came down to her firm, oversized, twenty-two-year bosoms. Her slim waist and enormous hips gave her the ideal hourglass figure. She wore an elegant, conservative blue gown that reached her ankle. The gorgeous young lady's buxom figure appeared to strain her dress requesting freedom from the restricting clothes.

Navin was born and brought up in the USA in a liberal family. He was the only son, as far as his parents were concerned. Like most typical Indian families, Navin had quite a number of relatives: uncles, aunts, cousins and distant brothers. However, not all of them were non-resident Indians like Navin and his family. They had been in the city of Los Angeles to attend a family wedding. Priya on the other had belonged to a very traditional and typical middle-class family in India. She had already gotten her admission in the Los Angeles Valley College and was in her mid-term semester back then. Her father was a friend of Navin's family and was invited to the USA to attend the wedding and that was where the two love birds met for the first time.

Priya may have been a conservative, intellectual, women's activist and a feminist at heart. But, on the most fundamental level, her body was that of the most sizzling stripper or porn star and Navin sensed there was a caged wild animal simply waiting

to be released underneath her cumbersome garments. Navin singled her out and eventually, she consented to go out with him. Priya and Navin had been just ready to see each other, hang out with each other, and party with each other after the college hours and on the weekends. They had been dating a year when she discovered Navin had a brother. Navin's mom, Maya, had one day just rolled her eyes and clarified how Kabir had dependably been the black sheep of the family. He had joined the Merchant Navy and after that invested his time and energy venturing into far away and distant lands on his cruiser doing unspecialized odd jobs all over, never staying in one spot for long, a typical wanderer.

Navin and Priya got married two years after meeting. At the time of their marriage, Navin was twenty-six years old and Priya twenty-three. Navin was 5'6" and extremely thin. His body was free from every possible ounce of fat, but then he didn't have any muscles either. She cherished him, loved him, and cared for him since Navin understood that marriage was an association and union of not only two souls, but also two families and he regarded her, treated her family with equal respect in every possible way. Navin had taken Priya's virginity on their wedding night and since that night and on countless nights he had been desperately attempting to loosen her up in bed. Navin couldn't get enough of her body and needed sex continually, which was a disgrace since Priya didn't appear to appreciate sex so much and could take it or leave it. Navin's fantasies were of oral and anal

sex, yet he could never get her past, beyond the age-old missionary style intercourse under the sheets with the lights out.

Navin had purchased a few porn movies having quite a number of distinct sexual encounters in a wide variety of positions, hoping that they would turn her on and give her ideas.

Priya had sat through the first video complaining about how it regarded women as objects and how offensive it seemed to be. Navin noticed Priya was absolutely mesmerized during a scene where a stud with a huge seven-inch cock was getting a blow job from a slutty, enormous breasted blonde. He looked over at her and discovered her gazing at the screen, her mouth dropping open in wonder and amazement. She had left for bed after that and Navin followed her after finishing the film. Perhaps, that was the first time Priya never complained about sex. Navin had climbed over her and inserted his thin four-and-a-half-inch penis into her married soaking wet pussy. They probably had the best sex of their marriage that night. However, all the desperate hopes and stimulating excitements of more of a kinkier, wilder wife never materialized for Navin, and Priya was reserved as usual.

To spice things up a little bit and relieve the boredom of same missionary position sex, Navin urged Priya to wear sultry outfits at parties. He relished the sight of every other man's eyes lurking on Priya's seductive curves; feasting on them like a pack

of hungry wolves. Priya was reluctant to wear something that to her seemed voyeuristic. After repeated pleadings from Navin, she decided to play along. She didn't trust her eyes or believe her senses at how successfully she aroused and seduce some men's minds and thoughts. Seeking the right tempting moment of joy and pleasure, Navin decided to bring in some role play based sex into the bedroom, and bingo it clicked more than anything. Lately, Navin always pleasured himself with cuckolding fetish role plays which to some extent were quite a turn on for Priya.

"Ohh haven't I… Well… Ah… Umm… I had…," Priya stopped as if unable to find words or perhaps unable to gather her senses from Navin's expert ministrations.

Navin unbuttoned her gown and slipped his hand inside grabbing a handful of her full-grown mammary glands, "You must have been sending him all the wrong signals. You're such a naughty wife." Priya squirmed at his touch, sighed, panted hard and chuckled.

"No, I am not. He's the one who is always ogling me. He's the one always desperate to make the first move," Priya sighed as goose bumps coursed over her glowing skin.

Navin kissed her boobs and flicked his tongue around her hardened nipples, "Keep talking. Don't stop."

"Well he cornered me in the storeroom today," she spoke. She could feel her heart beating like bass drums as a chilling wave gushed down her spine making her wet between her legs.

His cock sprang into life and was rock solid. Navin moaned and sucked hard on her nipples unable to resist the provocative temptation as his perverted mind crafted the image of an unfaithful wife.

"Why you seem to like it, don't you," Priya spoke stroking his cock.

"Tell me everything Priya. Tell me how naughty you were and what else he did to you," Navin grunted.

"Ouch!! Not so hard," Priya moaned grabbing his hand desperately trying to stop him from mauling her juicy tits so violently.

"Tell me," Navin gritted his teeth on one of her hardened nipples and pinched the other one harder.

"Uggg, Ahhh... he grabbed me in the storeroom during lunch hour... I was alone...," she forced Navin's head onto her breasts in a stimulating ecstasy which was buried in her breasts, perhaps sapped to it while caressing his balls.

"He pulled my top above my waist, kissed and sucked my navel. He fingered me from under my skirt without removing my

panties. I was so aroused. It was so wild. I was so tempted. Then he bent me over the table," Priya continued her story, "and positioned his long hard cock on my pussy by pulling aside the panties."

"Was he rough with you?" There was a note of desperation and excitement as Navin trembled at his own words.

"Yesss... he was very forceful. He forced his cock inside my pussy. I was about to scream in pain and pleasure. But he had muffled me with his palms." Priya sensed the excitement building in her rosebuds.

"Was he big? Bigger than your husband? Tell me you naughty girl," Navin almost pleaded as he continued showering his tongue tributes on her luscious tits.

"Mmmm... he was big and strong and he pinned me under him." Priya pushed Navin on the bed and climbed over him, she knew that she couldn't continue caressing his cock or he would cum in her hand. She guided his hard cock into her wet pussy and slid down on him.

"Ahhh... you're so hot and wet, ummm," Navin moaned as his cock felt the warmth of his wife's fertile pussy. Heaven, it was heaven on earth, or so Navin thought. Priya began to slowly move her ass and hips up and down on his erection and fuck him while continuing to tell her sensational fake story. Navin

was unable to take the seductive teasing for long and threw Priya on the bed and climbed over her.

"I'm going to fuck you so hard that your pussy will ache for weeks," Navin gritted his teeth and started to slam his cock into her. Priya closed her eyes and experienced the sensational ecstasy of a cuckolding role-play as she prepared herself to flow with the waves of the strong orgasm building inside her.

"Why don't you dare to do it for real," Navin spoke in a husky tone as they lay in each other's arms after the very satisfying and overwhelming orgasm.

"That was real," she teased him.

"Don't bullshit me... you are so sexy, gorgeous and filled with lust," Navin moved his hand across her nude lush frame, "any man would be willing to kill for you."

"I know that, but I don't want any bloodshed," Priya chuckled seductively.

Navin sighed because he knew this would remain one of his fantasies Priya would never take the leap of faith to experience it and make it happen for real.

"At least do it once," Navin pleaded, but looking at her smiling face, he realized that his words were all landing on deaf ears. But she was a thunderstorm wrapped in beautiful flesh, looking to

be felt and understood in a world that loved sunny days. Soon that storm overwhelmed her senses and turned her world upside down. And her best friend Becky just catalyzed her transformations.

As days turned into weeks and weeks into months, Priya started to wonder about Navin's proposals all the time. Priya and Navin worked in a reputed advertising company called Metric Theory and lived and maintained a very lavish and luxurious lifestyle.

They were team leaders in their respective fields; Priya in marketing and Navin in graphic designing. They could hardly complain about their salaries and perks; especially, when they were absolutely brilliant in their corporate roles.

They used to genuinely care for each other and their love knew no limits much like the kinkier side of Navin. They were the perfect match and "made for each other" type. If Navin was forgetful on any matter, Priya would step up to remind her husband what he was forgetting. If Navin would get too unsteady in the monthly finances, Priya would step up to hold the wallet. If Priya had a stressful day in office, Navin would step up to perform the household duties allowing Priya time to settle down and relax.

In every possible way, they complemented and filled each other. Needless to say about their kinkier and adventurous sides. Whenever they would make love, Navin would desperately plead

her to tell made-up stories about her stimulating adventures with her colleagues. This would be a huge turn on for Navin and he would always get the hardest erections he could ever imagine. As for Priya, although a pretense, she enjoyed her freedom and dominance that her husband's perverted fantasies allowed her.

Whenever Priya spent a relaxing evening alone getting her dinner, she couldn't stop pondering Navin's offer and the things that they had been talking about. It clearly rubbed her internal identity to feel that some other hunky men would find her attractive and tempting enough that they would actually want to fuck her. Throughout her married life, she had been absolutely faithful to Navin, but considering having sex outside her marriage was starting to turn her on.

She could feel her sensitive and delicate nipples beginning to rub against her blouse as they hardened at the very tempting thought. As she turned things over and over in her mind, she started to rationalize the situation. The more she thought about it, the more aroused she became. The more she imagined the circumstances, the more she started to justify to herself that if she was unfaithful with other men, then she would do it for Navin. She would grant her body to someone else to fulfill his perverted fantasies. The more she thought about it, the idea seemed to be increasingly captivating and she felt that it could be the perfect present for Navin's twenty-seventh birthday with the sole purpose that he could and would always remember his

birthday celebration. And besides, Navin always shared his kinky thoughts stating, "There is nothing sexier than watching men trying to catch a glimpse of my wife's bottom."

Sex Story 4: Concealed Games – Part 2

One day, Priya's fate took an upturn while she was deeply engaged in a lucrative project. Did any other colleague or office worker see what she saw? As she sat in front of the lit PC screen at her desk, her inquiring eyes would gravitate towards the strikingly hot male body that would frequently walk past her workstation. She was intensely aware of precisely where he was. His presence, Priya realized, was mesmerizing. She did her best to conceal any sign of her deepening interest. She'd never realized until that day how some men's magnetic personality could be so fascinating, or have such a mesmerizing way of leaving her feeling maddeningly stupid and shy; but then again, her experience of men was truly limited.

Priya never thought herself to be an unattractive girl, courtesy of the twisted fantasies of her perverted husband, Navin. However, she never truly grabbed the attention of young men like some of her female colleagues in the office did. She regularly thought about whether her lush body was too oversized, maybe even a little less pear shaped.

It was because of her reserved nature and typical Indian housewife mentality that she never quite felt she had the seductive tools to tease temptingly. In reality, she had no idea

that an alluring temptress was hiding beneath her clothes. Priya possessed a statuesque figure that often-made men's jaws fall open, especially, with a little encouragement from her deviant husband. She would wrap herself in some backless, sleeveless attire. Although Priya had a waist with a slight belly, she was fit and trim, and with growing age, she had gained her weight in perfect proportion, filling her body seductively; not to mention that her ass was well rounded, smooth, soft and firm showing off a spectacular booty. With gracious charm and an elegant smile, she always looked like fresh morning dew, carefully crafted by nature. But it was her juicy chest mounds that completely turned male heads.

Every year perfect proportions of weight and flesh were gained by those succulent breasts, gradually transforming them into an EE size that even the bra would find difficult to conceal. The way she accumulated her mass on her breast made them heavy, luscious, and jaw-dropping resembling pendulous udders hanging over her rib cage.

Priya found herself regularly looking at the tall, brawny body of a particular guy in the office, admiring how his elegant fitting clothing offered an engaging hint of what lay underneath. She cherished how his well-tailored shirts encased his torso in such a way that she could see his muscular arms.

"Ah, stop it," she would often confront her wild tempting thoughts. But then again, the rest of the time, she would give free reign to her provocative thoughts and imagined his arms encircling her. He undoubtedly worked out. That she could tell right away. He had that solid Herculean manliness she found so incredibly appealing.

For a long time, whenever he spoke to Priya, all she could manage to utter was a fairly chocked hi, or an inane response to his pleasant, enchanting inquiries and greetings. Just replying with a few pleasantries made Priya blush and she stumbled on her words.

"Why did he need work here at my first and most significant position in the office since leaving College?" Priya desperately wondered. Throughout the next few days, after she got her promotion in this dynamic advertising company: Metric Theory, she didn't get caught up in the glamour of the corporate world. Instead, she ended up awfully focused on her immediate boss, the fantastically hot Dominic Tucker.

Priya expected to discover another distraction in the workplace. She was becoming enthralled by him. "What's so special about this man? Is it his position of power that makes him a real alpha in the office? Is it his brawny Herculean black body that captures my attention?" Priya wondered, clueless, without any proper answers. Being her immediate boss brought about a level

of fascination for her. His success was surely a factor. His charisma to appeared to be his command of every situation, unlike herself, who could only be described as a team leader of the marketing team. In spite of the fact that she thought she was extremely good at her job; she couldn't resist thinking that she was exceeding expectations of being absolutely besotted by the man who was her manager. A little cliché, but there you have it.

Dominic was irresistible to Priya. There was one other thing that attracted her more than she suspected- his delightful dark bronze skin. She had never been with a black man before.

Actually, she'd never been much into men and Navin was the only man in her life both before and after marriage. However, with Dominic, his dark skin was inserted into her sexual images of him and her like no other fantasies. She imagined his exquisite blackness against her light brown Indian shade.

One day, Priya mustered all her courage despite her heart beating like bass drums and took the bold initiative to invite the man of her erotic dreams, Dominic, to her house to attend her husband Navin's birthday party. Surely, Dominic was not a man to turn down his seductive assistant's offer. Especially, when he had already sensed Priya's underlying crush and heightened interest.

When Dominic reached Priya's home, he was astounded to find a lively party going on. It was an absolutely magical

environment. Dominic, though the center of attraction of the party as far as Priya was concerned, found himself in a little bit of an awkward situation among most of the Indian guests.

The moon glowed like a glittering disco ball and shone all through the night. The vibrant glow of the lighting decorations added to the festive atmosphere of the room which held the main event. Loud DJ music played hit songs non-stop. There were ample drinks that provided a warm welcome to all the guests.

Gradually, the awkward silences in Dominic's mind and heart faded away and he started to feel at home. After a few drinks, he relaxed and even posed for some pictures with the fellow party attendees.

Navin, the birthday boy was looking exceptionally smart and handsome in his black tuxedo. Priya looked like an angel from heaven in her traditional Indian dress silk sari. The sari was elegant and of bright colorful shades matching the electrifying excitement and stimulating temptations in Priya's mind. Her top was sleeveless with deep décolletage showing off her tempting cleavage. The backless design to her traditional dress was enough to provoke impure thoughts in all the male party attendees, especially Dominic's.

Priya wore a matching pair of red Madden Girl Peep-Toe high heels exhibiting the new anklet she wore that evening.

Her overall look was immensly captivating. She wore a delicate white gold necklace with a diamond pendant that fell at her enticing cleavage. It matched her bangle earrings.

"Wow! You look hot! So perfect," Navin teased Priya in the middle of the party.

"Yes, I know. And I hope you'll love your birthday present as well." Priya teased back.

"Wait, what present?" Navin questioned back as his heart beat faster.

"Surprise! It won't be a surprise if I tell you." Priya winked and went on to check on the guests.

"These are the advantages of being married to an absolute knockout!" Navin thought with pride.

Dominic complimented Priya on her elegantly graceful look and told her how dazzling she looked. They were constantly exchanging glances at each other throughout the party.

At one point, Navin noticed that there was an odd tension building between Dominic and Priya. Priya was really quiet when she got close to Dominic. But she made sure to send all the tempting indications like showing off her cleavage, her belly button, even her big bubble butts to Dominic to entice him. As the party progressed, the attendees helped themselves to the

exquisite Indian dishes and wine and couldn't stop praising the flavorsome items. This was when Dominic cracked some silly jokes to lighten Priya's mood which made her giggle. But, Navin, Priya, and Dominic never appeared to be too keen on eating.

By 9:30 in the evening, all of the guests had left leaving only the three of them, Dominic, Priya, and Navin. Dominic was amazed when Priya sat close to him on the couch. He gazed at her and found an incredibly hot wife, wrapped in an exquisite sari. Her long hair was flawlessly tied behind her neck, reaching down her waist. The Sari was well beneath the belly button. Her seductive curvy abdomen showed, while her juicy boobs looked ready to blast out of their confinements.

Priya was sitting close enough to Dominic that he could smell her sweet perfume. He had a magazine on his lap, but it lay unopened as his attention was focused on their conversation. She showed him pictures of her family, her in-laws and some picnic photos she had on her phone. He talked about his job and she showed interest while telling him about her family in India and married life in Los Angeles.

Dominic glanced at her husband and found a normal looking young fellow immersed in a book and giving little consideration to his better half.

Dominic was not complaining, "It means that either this woman is really talkative and dumb or she is stuck in a frustrating

marriage with this guy." Dominic wondered. He too showed photos of his family and distant relatives and kept on connecting with her in talk.

Navin was unable to understand Priya's behavior. She had never done this before and he didn't have the faintest idea how to react. All of a sudden, his heart jumped out of his chest when he saw Priya lean into Dominic showing him something and her naked shoulder brushed against his. He saw that she didn't draw back. Instead she kept it squeezed against him while continuing with her animated explanations about the photo.

Dominic felt energized; his cock grew in size and was making a tent in his trousers. He discreetly balanced the magazine on his lap and looked at Priya with wonder as she slipped nearer to him and let her body to touch his. "What's happening with her? Is she playing with this man regardless of my presence? Has she chosen to make my dream a reality?"

Navin's mind crowded with all sorts of twisted questions as he rationalized the situation while looking surreptitiously at the duo. Navin examined the black hunk. He had all the exquisite qualities of a bodybuilder and appeared older than he yet was fit as a fiddle. Dominic was not shy to deviate himself from such a tempting situation and manly self-arrogant gleams emanated from his face as he chuckled at Navin. Navin felt his gut wrench.

After a while, Dominic excused himself to take a leak. "Is this lady coming on to me or is she only a talkative flirtatious woman stuck with a boring spouse?" Dominic wondered, "She may not realize that she's sending a wide range of wrong signals which can make any man slip."

When Dominic left the room, Navin set his book aside and looked at Priya dubiously. He was puzzled. This Priya, he knew all along was different. Priya grinned mysteriously.

"What is this?" Navin enquired.

She strolled enticingly towards him, "Isn't this what you always desperately asked for."

Navin nodded stupidly.

"Well, I have decided to fulfill your fantasy," she murmured seductively. Her, smell, her voice, her eyes, her face was brimming with confidence never seen before.

"But... but..." Navin stammered, "He is so terrible, and he's black, I don't want him to be your lover." He made an awful face.

"He is a lot fitter than you. Besides, it's me who will sleep with him, not you. So I get to choose my men."

Navin was stunned, speechless, petrified at her blatant reply. All of a sudden, she began to chuckle hysterically. He looked at her

without a clue while she kept on snickering and then she embraced him firmly.

"Oh! My sweet husband," Priya crushed him against her juicy bosom, "I just wanted to give you a genuine feel of your twisted fantasy. How did you feel when I was getting comfortable with him?" Navin struggled to find words as he froze in fear. He had no idea how and what to respond. He just licked his parched lips and gulped.

"I realized you would back down if I ever attempt it in reality," Priya kept on chuckling.

"No... no... I didn't back down... it's simply that this man is not my sort." Navin trembled with excitement as he replied.

"Well, I told you already. I am the one picking the person and I have picked him," she grinned seductively, "You will always be unable to approve any man I pick. That is the reason my sweetheart... it is best that you let your fantasy remain fantasy."

"Of course sweetheart, you can pick... it's simply that I was overwhelmed," Navin understood that Priya was prodding him and he sensed the stimulating thrill, "Would you do it?"

"We will see," Priya chuckled mischievously and touched his crotch, "Oh! My god, you are so hard already," she laughed.

"Please do it," after the initial shock, Navin was feeling the thrill once more.

"Then, my dear husband, I want you to allow me to have him in my way so I can give you a thrill." Priya was serious.

"Okay! As you wish." Navin gulped. Before he could process anything more, he felt his alluring wife's luscious lips crashing on his parched lips. Navin was powerless even to respond and he felt Priya's tongue and lips swirling in his mouth and over his lips. All Navin felt was the fire burning in Priya; the fire of her seduction; the fire of her lust that was consuming her.

The discussion ended as they heard Dominic's footsteps in the corridor. He was carrying three bottles of beer, one for each of them.

Priya put on a Hindi movie on the DVD player. It was about a romantic affair brimming with passionate romantic tunes.

There were intermittent thunder and lightning flashes that caught Navin's eye through the blinds. A storm was about to come. But, Navin was not sure whether the storm was imminent in his house or outside.

Suddenly, his phone buzzed and he had to check it even when his mind was busy crafting his twisted fantasies. It was a call from his director requesting a paper edit ASAP. "Come on, this is my birthday!" His mind was yelling at his boss, but he knew

what a lucrative project he'd been working on these last few months. So, Navin excused himself to work from the library.

Meanwhile, Priya and Dominic cuddled up in the lounge chair under a blanket since they were both a bit cold. There was no time for Priya to question her activities as Dominic's mouth squeezed hard against hers and she felt the power of his muscular frame as he leaned onto her.

Priya lost all her inhibitions and let those long stretches of provocative sexual interest that had been brewing at her desk appear in full force. Her arms wrapped around his neck. Priya couldn't get them to move quickly enough around his torso, up and down his chest, around and down onto his muscular hips. Dominic, in turn, reacted with equal passion, giving his hands a chance to move seductively to explore her lush body.

Priya's hands came down and felt the lump in his pants. She was desperate to devour his muscular body, to work her way over the tight dark skin of his chest, to press her body against his with her arms wrapped around those unimaginable muscular ass cheeks.

The calm, shy attitude was a distant memory as Priya let herself flow and could feel the wild passion that had been raging in her mind explode upon him, and there she was, claiming him for herself.

Navin hurried through his work half-assed as he couldn't think straight and his mind was crowded with all sorts of twisted fantasies of watching his wife with another man. He was desperate to meet his wife and her new lover and completed the paperwork by 11:30 pm.

When Navin returned to the living room with another three bottles of beer, he saw Priya and Dominic kissing passionately. Navin felt his heart beating like bass drums. This was so unexpected and far wilder and raw - absolutely catching him off guard! The romantic duo saw Navin and broke the kiss and readjusted them. Each of them felt extremely awkward.

They pretended nothing had happened, although Navin felt his organ getting hard at the mere sight to see his legally wedded wife in another man's arms. To alleviate the awkward silence and tension, Dominic attempted to start a discussion.

"Hey Navin, did you know Priya is a great romantic dancer?" Dominic teased.

Priya rolled her eyes and shrugged to dismiss the comments, "Yeah, right! Stop joking around!"

"Really," Navin looked surprised and amused.

"I'm not kidding Navin! We were talking about this romantic song and I remembered how your wife shook her hips to its beat at an office party. She really made some girls in my office jealous

with her captivating and enchanting moves." Dominic was serious.

"Is that so? Well, give me a chance to relive that moment!" Navin winked at Priya.

Priya traded looks with Dominic and then with Navin. It was evident that neither of them was going to rescue her.

Priya complained, "This is stupid guys. I'm not doing this." Then turning towards Dominic, "And you, you just finish the movie and then we're done."

Navin ignored Priya and raised the volume of the DVD. The beats were filled with rhythmic variety and fabulous musical stimulation, yet, none of them would move. Navin stopped it and wickedly looked at his wife, waiting patiently.

Dominic stood up, stretched out his hands to Priya and approached her for the moves. Priya looked up and grinned at him. Reluctantly she stood up and began shaking her hips. It was gentle and not a very up-close dance. But since the song involved a titillating booty move, Navin was excited and felt his erection poking his pants. Her provocative dress raised the bar a notch higher. The manner in which she shook her wide ass, her smooth thighs, and bounced her luscious and juicy tits was enough to make any man cum in his pants.

Dominic's passion was gradually inflamed, taking it to the point of no return. He was the sole manipulator in complete control of the circumstances. The raging thunderstorm outside had made it significantly more passionate. This was the first time that Navin was seeing them together. Strangely, he felt less jealous than he suspected he'd feel. He was in a condition of electrifying excitement and animated expectation.

After the song ended, Navin asked if they wanted to dance some more? It looked like what had begun reluctantly had now gotten their juices streaming. Priya looked at Dominic for some time, and it seemed as if she was gazing at her own reflection in his eyes. They had no reactions whatsoever and after a while, Priya nodded her approval. Navin put on some erotic jazz music this time. Initially, the romantic duo kept a distance just holding each other's hand. Then, Priya held her hands over her head and gradually swung her hips.

"God, that's awesome. I always knew my gorgeous wife was hiding such a wild spirit in her," Navin thought as he felt his erection twitch at his significant other's alluring abilities residing in her stunning bottom.

The romantic duo turned towards one another and gradually Priya surrendered to a passionate embrace. She snaked her hands behind Dominic's neck tightly, pressing her juicy breasts against his chest and looking into his eyes. It was strange for

Navin to watch his legally wedded wife taking a lover right in front of him. A peculiar blend of pain and passion conquered his feelings as he felt lost in the realm of his own twisted fantasies. Compared to his pounding heartbeat, the loud jazz music felt calm.

They continued moving and Navin's marvelous wife crushed her groin against Dominic's jeans. Dominic turned her around and held her waist from the back and they continued dancing. Priya was breathing hard and thrusting her hips to the rhythmic beat.

Her eyes were shut and her mouth partially open! Dominic kissed her behind her ears and was teasing her neck and shoulders.

Priya gazed at Navin once in a vulnerable and powerless stupor and then shut her eyes once again. Something in Navin's eyes assured Priya of their marriage vows. Her mouth was gradually opening wider as she let her lust conquer her senses. Her dress was disheveled from the intensified grinding and the wild movement of her hips.

It felt like forever and none of them wanted this to end. The duo continued dancing song after song. Navin didn't stop them in this state and they, for the most part, ignored him.

At long last the playlist ended dragging them back to reality. It was close to 1:00 am. The sounds of the storm finally came to their notice.

Priya took a couple of steps forward, approached Navin and sat on his lap. Dominic came too and sat on the opposite armchair. Priya looked into her husband's eyes with concern. One of the advantages of being married to a lady for quite a long time is that you figure out how to communicate with your eyes. Navin and Priya were no exception. She kissed him and afterward bit her luscious lips and looked seductively. Navin realized what she was asking for. She was requesting his permission to fulfill his twisted fantasies. She was burning in wild lust as it consumed her senses. She'd just moistened between her legs.

Navin was an expert to sense the seductive temptations in his wife. He nodded, kissed her and gave her a wicked smile. That was it. The stage was set for Priya and Dominic.

It was now all on Dominic as to how like an alpha he would make his last move. Priya asked if Navin had loved her dancing. When Navin said, "I did," she became flushed. Her skin felt sticky. Her intensifying sexual fragrance was overtaking her flowery perfume.

Just then, the power went out. It was truly dark, yet the lightening from the storm matched the raging storm inside their hearts.

Navin used his cell phone to get to the kitchen and began lighting a few candles. He asked if they could put a few candles in the living room while he went to check the circuit panel. They obliged.

Navin attempted to fix the breaker; however, it seemed the entire neighborhood was out. When Navin returned to the living room, what he discovered excited him.

All the teasing throughout the evening and the illicit idea of fulfilling her husband's deviant fantasies had made Priya incredibly horny. Dominic was mauling her juicy bosoms over the blouse and was squeezing them hard. When Priya opened her mouth, Dominic kissed her passionately. She darted her tongue forward and let him suck it. She arched her body in agony and moaned as he pinched and kneaded her hardened nipples.

She stared at Navin, and even in the candlelight, Priya sensed he had his eyes fixed on her as though begging her to cuckold him. She could even now feel the flavor of Dominic's tongue and the powerful rough hands that ravaged her juicy tits; a shivering sensation kept running between her legs.

Navin was nervously squirming; even in the candle lights, he could unmistakably observe her and her expressions were undermining him, threatening him. "Will she do it? Is he going

to take the final leap?" Navin was trembling with excitement, waiting patiently, in anticipation.

It seemed like hours before he finally saw some development. Priya pushed Dominic on the couch as she freed herself from his strong embrace. She was standing in front of Dominic, and behind him was her legal husband, Navin. Navin watched in sheer surprise as Priya started to remove her sari. He couldn't see, yet he knew Dominic was on the couch feasting on every curve of his Indian wife. His heart leaped as she tossed the Sari to the floor, next came her top and Priya was standing in front of Dominic in just her panties. This was really happening, this was so real and yes, Priya was going to fuck this man. "My better half would be taken by this man," it dawned on Navin and it hit him hard. His body trembled, partly in pain, but mostly in excitement. Dominic tried to get up, but Priya set a firm hand on his chest and pushed him back on the seat. Dominic said something in a murmur which Navin was unable to hear and Priya chuckled deviously.

Her nipples were hard to the point of aching and they had come to life for the first time in years, becoming agonizingly sensitive.

Priya gradually became mindful of the dampness between her legs. No, they weren't simply moist; her panties were soaked through to the point where she was dripping through the fine silken fabric. "Why is this exciting me?" Priya wondered in

absolute shock. She was all the while keeping Dominic down with one hand when he was attempted to move toward her again. So she put both her hands on his chest.

Dominic seized the moment cupped her breasts. They were an absolutely mesmerizing sight to see.

"Sorry Priya, I couldn't help myself," Dominic apologized despite the fact that his body was all the while attempting to embrace her.

Her own hands were sliding over the hard pectorals on his chest. "Goodness," Priya thought, "this is one solid muscular chest." Priya started to undress her lover and soon Dominic was just in his boxers resting on the couch with his clothes lying next to Priya's sari on the floor. Priya looked at his hard six pack abs. She'd never seen him shirtless and was awestruck by his physical fitness.

Priya gazed at him and knelt down before him. She couldn't bring herself to gaze at his groin. Rather, she gazed at Dominic's fit torso. "Take it out," Priya requested.

"You take it out," Dominic grunted.

Priya moaned, looking at his shorts, long enough for her hand to discover the edge. She turned away again as she pulled away his boxers and reached in with her other hand. She felt his pubic

hair, and her hand grabbed the base of what felt like a human wrist.

"What the heck is that?" she asked herself, sliding her hand down the hot, hard as a steel shaft. Her fingers didn't even encircle it, it was so thick. It was caught by his shorts so Priya pulled them further and down as her hand liberated the mammoth dark big black cock from its confinement.

"OH MY GOD!" she screamed in sheer shock, her black eyes going cross-eyed as she gazed at what must be an enormous foot long black cock. The head was lighter than the pole which was filled with thick blue-black veins, pulsating with wild lust and life. She'd never seen anything like this before.

Priya gazed at it in shock, lifting the pole up over her head. She adjusted her eyes in a futile attempt to bring the entire thing into better focus. "I've never seen anything so huge," she stated, still gazing in absolute wonder.

"It's about normal for a black man." Dominic enjoyed the naïve way she was gazing at it.

"Navin isn't even half as long or as thick," Priya stated.

"I felt bad for ya," Dominic answered. "I could sense that you've faked the vast majority of your bedtime climaxes."

Priya released the gigantic black shaft and it fell forward to point directly at her mouth sticking out over the hem of his shorts. She brought her lips near the bulbous head of his big black hardened cock.

Dominic asserted, "You'll be the first Indian lady to ever suck on it or taste it."

For reasons unknown, Priya felt fortunate to be the first Indian lady to suck such a splendid erection of a potent man. She desperately wished that she had more practice.

"I haven't done this for Navin in the past couple of months," she thought, stretching her mouth open and taking the bulbous head into her mouth. She looked at her wedding ring on her hand, but the lust that possessed her never let her consider her marriage vows. More so, when it was her husband who provoked her fantasies to serve other men.

"DAYUMN!" the Herculean hunk, snorted once, his whole-body trembling in passionate excitement. Priya grabbed his thighs through his shorts to steady him as she began bobbing her head around the tip of his monster penis. "Your mouth is so hot! It feels so damn good," Dominic exclaimed with wonder and disbelief.

Priya let her tongue slurp around the tip before bobbing her head once more. Luckily, for Priya, her expertise in blowjobs

hadn't faded away and Dominic was getting excited from the very beginning. Perhaps all the seductive temptations throughout the evening had brought him to the threshold of a stimulating orgasm.

"Just wait until you discover how tight and hot my married pussy is?" Priya thought as she peered directly into his eyes. Speaking of married pussies, hers was aching with a desperate urge, and overwhelming want. Dominic was standing firm now, so Priya pulled one hand off his shorts and moved it down to her pussy. Her fingers pushed the fine silken fabric of the panties aside and slid into the warm and moistened folds of her wet pussy. "So horny," she thought, fingering herself with her middle finger. Her pussy drenched the rest of her fingers to her wrist. She was so wet.

As for Navin, he stood at the living room threshold, in the dark, watching in sheer lust and a strange horror his wife slurping on a big black cock while fingering herself. He watched his conservative Indian wife breaking the vows of Orthodox marriage.

For a moment, Priya stared at the doorway. She made out the dark shadowy figure in the dull light. She never knew that being watched while having sex could be such huge arousal for her. Navin felt hurt, his face was contorted as looked in her eyes in the candlelight. He found it hard to breathe. His mind was in a

weird fusion of terrible agony and electrifying excitement. He wanted to say something but his voice betrayed him.

Her body's response was absolutely amazing and all the more astounding as Priya felt tremors inside her pussy. "Going to cum," she thought with dismay even as she squirted all around her finger. "Why am I enjoying this so much?" Priya thought with a pang of irrational guilt even as she worked her finger as fast as she could to extend the most overwhelming climax she'd ever experienced.

Priya pushed forward, his bulbous cock head, pushing past her uvula and ramming down her throat. This was way further than her Indian husband's pin dick had ever gone when she had blown him and Dominic's was stretching her throat much further. She groaned around his gigantic, monstrous erection, embarrassed by how excited she was getting sucking this huge black cock. Priya inhaled deeply and took as much of the marvelous erection down her throat as she could, his pubes coming nearer to her nose. However, it was too much and Priya yanked her head back before she started to choke and gasped for air.

Dominic's mammoth erection rose up, glistening from her saliva. Priya held the base of the splendid organ, caressing it while she brought her left hand up and held the alpha's full dark gonads. Priya always thought she'd had a decent sex life with

Navin, at least some of the time. Now she felt bamboozled. The gonad in her grasp was as large as a tennis ball and heavier. Navin's little nuts resembled grapes in comparison to this black Hercules.

Dominic sat down on the edge of the couch and laid back. Priya moved between his legs and took his magnificent erection in her mouth. One hand held his cock while she sucked him. Her other hand reached down behind her and slid over her rear end to her horny pussy. However, she stopped caressing herself once more. Dominic's stamina was amazing. Eventually, his shaft started swelling up. "Suck it, slut," he groaned. "GONNA CUM!"

Priya's bosoms were standing out between his thighs, so she sat up and heaved her bosoms in his lap until they wrapped around his mammoth shaft. Priya sucked the head of his erection hard. It was now gigantic and difficult to get down her throat. It jerked once and her mouth was brimming with cum to the point her cheeks bulged and sperm splashed away from around her luscious lips. "So much cum," Priya thought in dismay. She swallowed, yet her mouth filled over and over with every spasm of his big black cock. Priya was choking on sperm to the point where she needed to pull back. His gigantic shaft was hosing her mouth and cheeks with semen. She gazed down at his pole, pressing it between her juicy bosoms. Stream after stream of thick white sperm shot up from the head, tumbling down to coat his mammoth black pole and her luscious udders with his seed.

The squirts stopped, but the sperm kept oozing from the head to run down his pole. Priya was desperate for another taste and took him back in her mouth; her tongue devouring up all the potent protein juices coating the big black cock.

Navin was bewildered at what he was witnessing. He couldn't make out which storm was more violent, the one raging outside or the one raging inside his living room turning his world upside down. This was an absolutely new avatar that he witnessed in his wife. He knew she had a wild side, but never expected it to overwhelm his senses. He stared helplessly at the sky as his twisted fantasies turned into reality step by step.

Concealed Games – Part 3

Priya quietly stood and licked her lips. Dominic's erection smacked down on his stomach, remaining a Goliath, yet losing its hardness. She gradually turned and went to the washroom to clean up. As she walked past her husband, her eyes blazed with a passion and wild lust that Navin had rarely seen before. Navin tried to say something, but her casual attitude toward him stopped him. He could only step away from the Goddess of lust walking past him. Navin was already rock hard and all the time his little dick twitched as he watched his wife serving a big black cock with ardent fervor and passion. He hadn't even touched his organ, yet he was on the threshold of an electrifying blast. Navin followed his wife into the bathroom lighting her way with a candle. The power had been out for over an hour now.

Priya leaned over the sink and turned the hot water tap on. Her nipples and ample bosoms were dribbling with the black man's cum to the point that semen was trickling off her nipples into her sink.

Priya had sometimes swallowed for Navin, but she hardly cared for the taste. Dominic was unique. His sperm had tasted incredibly great. Awesome! So great, she was desperate for more. Priya hefted her bosom and brought her nipple up to her mouth. The spasm that shook her lush body when her tongue hit

her erect nipple had her pussy leaking once more. They had truly come to life like a volcano after being dormant for so long. She licked her other nipple clean, her desire growing each time her tongue flickered over the hard nub. Dominic's seed tasted so great, although it was cold now and she favored it hot and fresh spurting out of his big black cock. "Perhaps, he'll let me suck him again," Priya wondered, astonishing herself and now wanting more of his seed.

Navin watched in sheer disbelief as his wife licked the last residue of the protein juices from her ample breasts. "What is happening to me? What has happened to Priya?" He questioned himself desperately seeking an answer.

Priya cleaned herself up and brushed her teeth.

Finally, she walked seductively toward her pimp husband Navin and caressed his cheek as if he were a child.

"Hey..." Priya said so quietly nearly inaudible to the human ear.

"Hey..." Navin responded as he heard the seductive temptress talking to him for the first time in over an hour.

Priya made an "Oh my gosh!" face... and then made a serious face looking at him...

Priya embraced Navin and he trembled like a dry leaf in a whirlwind. Then, she breathed into his ears, "Are you mad at me

hon? This time, I really put you between a rock and a hard place, didn't I?"

"No my love…" Navin gulped.

Navin smiled, unable to find words to express his feelings for his newly discovered wife. Priya smiled back… She just kept gazing at him intensely…

"Can I ask you a little favor?" Her voice was serious.

"Sure baby… Whatever you want," Navin licked his parched lips.

"Promise you won't get mad?" Her intent was absolute.

"Promise…" Navin couldn't help but surrender.

"Can you please sleep in the guest bedroom? I mean… I don't know… this is umm…" Priya couldn't finish her words and Navin interrupted her with a passionate kiss. He could still smell the pungent smell of the black sperm that overwhelmed his wife's mouth. "Don't worry babe I understand," was his honest approval.

"I will make it up to you. I promise!" Priya winked and released him of her embrace as if he never existed. For a moment, Navin felt his heart sinking. A while ago, he was so excited to have his wife back in his arms and now within a few moments, she was out of his reach again.

When Priya entered the living room, Dominic sat up like a king waiting for his queen, his stout monstrous organ slapping over his leg. "I figured I should return you the favor," he asserted.

Dominic slid off the couch so that he could kneel before Priya, his face gazing at the purple panty completely drenched with her own juices. His hand caressed her thigh.

Navin saw two pitch black hands grabbing Priya by her waist. He watched in sheer horror as the huge hands grabbed the silken panties and pulled them apart, 'snap' the elastic broke and the fabric was torn in two. Dominic tossed it over the heap of garments and his hands were all over her exposed rear end. Navin heard Priya pant in excitement; her eyes were wide open as she looked past him.

Priya began trembling as her juicy rosebuds gave a little squirt. "It's been such a long time," she gasped.

"Just let me pleasure you," Dominic stated, sticking his tongue out.

Dominic teased Priya for a little while as he snaked his tongue across her inner thighs, licking the flavorsome juice dripping out of her rosebuds. Then, he simply planted his mouth directly on her groin and inserted his tongue into her wet pussy.

"YES!" cried Priya, spasms of delightful ecstasy racking her body as goosebumps coursed through her glowing skin. "Wiggle your

tongue, yes! Just like that! Oh, My GOD!" She grabbed his head and pulled him hard into her groin. Priya had relished getting eaten practically more than she enjoyed sex and Navin had been superbly great at it. God, she'd missed this. "That is great Dominic," she groaned, "eat my pussy."

Dominic ceased for a moment, but just long enough to turn Priya so that she was well settled on the couch. She screeched with ecstatic joy when his tongue came back to her clit and didn't stop as she had lost herself in overwhelming wild lust. He flicked his tongue over her swollen clit, ravishing the beauty of the rosebud before pushing his fingers into her.

"Aaaaah!" groaned Priya as Dominic's finger fucked her. "That's it," she screeched. Her body was trembling once more. "Good GOD!" Her legs shook and became powerless. "Going to CUM!" Her legs gave out and Priya arched on the chair, spreading her legs wide for her man of the hour. Dominic's fingers popped out. He grabbed her ass and lifted her whole lower body up off the couch, her legs twisting around his head as he buried his face in her wet pussy working his tongue as quickly as possible.

"AAAHHH!" shouted Priya, loudly. The sound of her screams pierced Navin's heart and he felt his little pin dick twitching as he heard his wife moaning hard, "I am CUMMING!" Her pussy squirted all over Dominic's face, drenching his cheeks and jaw. She'd never cum so hard and his squirming tongue kept

devouring her pussy making it not only the greatest, but also the longest climax she had ever experienced.

Dominic stood and wiped the back of his hand over his face. Priya turned her head and grinned seductively at him, watching his huge donkey cock swinging as he hopped onto the couch and settled down on it. Priya moved to lie next to him leaning toward him as the two of them caught their breaths. She ran her hand over his chest, appreciating his musculature. "How long has it been since I had two climaxes?" Priya asked herself. Her hand slid over Dominic's black muscular abs. "One today, but months, a year?" Her mind was corrupted by sinful lust.

"You're so natural Dominic," she let him know. Her hand went down over his stomach and grabbed his fat flaccid black shaft, stroking it. Very quickly, her fingers opened as the cock hardened gaining its strength at the touch of a tempting hot wife.

"It seems that it's getting hard again," Dominic stated, caressing Priya's naked back. Priya sat up. His mammoth erection had regained its hardness and full length now and her hand was stroking it. She gazed at it; she licked her parched lips as she prepared to suck him once more. "I want to fuck you. I'm so desperate to have you completely," he moaned.

Navin's cock twitched once again as he witnessed his wife getting conquered by a more potent man. Priya's pussy let out

another little squirt. Her body clearly loved the attention she was receiving, and her mind was completely lost in the desire for the enormous dark shaft in her grasp. She leaned down drawing her mouth closer to his delightful veiny pole.

"Slide your pussy on my cock," Dominic commanded. He was going to finally claim his prize.

"Please be careful, Dominic. My husband is not even thrice the length of this cock," Priya looked at the monstrous black cock in her grasp. She truly wanted to suck it once more; however, Dominic's command lured her.

Priya sucked her lower lip in eagerness to feel his hot shaft throbbing between her legs. She straddled his waist and brought herself down over his pole. Her labia spread out around the base of his erection oozing her lustful excitement and drenching his hardened shaft. She drove her groin down onto his pole, groaning as she felt his hot and fully erect big black cock throbbing with life.

Navin leaned against the wall as the strength in his legs gave way. He couldn't move. "This is my dream, my most desired fantasy," he thought, "Then why am I feeling ashamed of it? In my dream, she was constantly fucked hard and she generally enjoyed the other man's cock, so what's up now?" Navin was desperate to search for an answer.

He was unable to continue looking at his slutty wife, the very same girl whom he loved and married and whose virginity he took. The realization was truly heart wrenching for him; he averted his eyes. But he couldn't do it for long as the excitement was too wild to deny. "The acknowledgment that your wife needs another man hits hard and it hurts. The other man fucking is making her scream in ecstasy and moaning in profound joy." Navin wondered. He felt wave after wave of envy as each of Dominic's thrusts slammed into his wife's pussy. But then his pin dick was hard. He'd never heard such loud moans from his wife and they were intensifying in volume. He had never heard her scream and moan so hard in pleasure.

Priya slid up and down the base of his black erection, increasing her speed.

"YES!" she groaned as his hips slapped her ample ass. Her bosoms shook rhythmically as she worked her pussy along the entire length of his mammoth erection.

In the candlelight, Navin watched in disbelief as he witnessed a big black cock disappearing into his wife's married Indian cunt, conquering her, claiming her and abusing her very hole which he once proudly owned.

Priya had never seen her nipples so engorged. They stood out more than half an inch and her areola were puffed out as well making the end of her nipples stick out nearly a full inch.

Dominic wasn't, looking at her. His arms were under his head, eyes shut, with a marvelous look on his face. He groaned, raising his hip to her, lazily opening his eyes, opening more extensively at the delightful sight of her bosoms dancing rhythmically in front of his face with every thrust. Dominic reached up and squeezed both her nipples. Waves of profound blissful joy rippled through her body at his touch.

Behaving like a slut in a way she never had for him, Navin couldn't believe it when Priya who begged Dominic to fuck her tight hole! She was reacting as if she was possessed by a demon. As a matter of fact, she was possessed by the demon of her own buried lust. Navin watched in awe as this huge muscled man reached up and kissed his wife! She ran her delicate hands over his chiseled body as his huge cock penetrated her deeper than Navin ever could. The scene was too much for Navin to keep watching and he retreated to his room. Yet his mind kept on playing with his senses as his wife enjoyed fucking Dominic.

"I want to mark you as my bitch," Dominic whispered. Priya looked absolutely puzzled.

"I'll leave my mark on you so that when you see those marks you'll remember who made them," he groaned and dug his teeth deep with full force on her delicate luscious udder.

"AHHHHHHHHHH... AAUUUUCCCHHHH...
AHHHHHHHHHH." Priya screamed in an ecstatic blend of pain and pleasure.

Her eyes opened wide as she pushed him back desperately grabbing his hairs. But his strong teeth dug deep into the flesh of her succulent udders and stayed there. A sharp agony rushed through her body; a tingling effect flooded through her spine as goosebumps coursed through her entire lush skin. Priya kicked her legs in unbearable agony, but Dominic kept sucking with his teeth dug deep into her flesh. After a while, her body got used to the pain and then a sensational stirring effect flowed from her nipples overpowering her pussy. She bucked her groin and held his head tightly pressed over her succulent udders wanting him more than ever before.

"Now, I'm going to mark the other tit," Dominic groaned, taking the succulent boob in his mouth.

"Ummm... AHHH..." Priya felt an orgasm growing inside her married womanhood and she was desperate to cross the threshold of her sensational passionate excitements. Priya groaned louder even before Dominic had placed his mouth over her right breast.

"AHHHHHHHHHH... AAAAUUUCCHHH... OHHHHHHHHHH," Priya screamed out loud once again grasping his hairs. She gasped loudly, nearly breathless to endure the pain waiting for it

to recede; but the thrilling sensation began to shoot electric thunders deep inside her pussy.

Priya worked her hips harder and faster, sliding along the entire length of his big black cock. She looked down between the gullies of her bosoms and witnessed the end of his mammoth shaft standing out from her groin. This black Herculean man's enormous pole delivered more lube than her husband's whole climax, a few times over; however, then it would take a great deal to coat such an immense weapon. Indeed, even as she gazed, another sticky load oozed from the head of his cock. Her married Indian cunt was milking his big black cock.

Her pussy was sliding closer to the head now, and she began concentrating on the end of his shaft over the base of his pole. Her pussy lips spread out around the head and Priya's body shook with desire when another stream of his precum struck her swollen clit. Priya whimpered in desire, feeling the head half lodged at the passage to her pussy. All she needed to do was push down and back and his shaft would be inside her. Priya was nearing her orgasm again and realized that would work, but still, she controlled herself.

Priya propelled herself up off the pole, yet his erection rose up with her; the head as yet spreading her lips separated while in the meantime, Dominic sat up and sucked one of her engorged

nipples between his lips. That was all it took to set her off. "I'M CUMMING AGAIN!" Priya screamed in ecstasy.

Floods of liquid splashed his cock head and kept running down his pole. It didn't require any more liquid. However, the additional lubrication coupled with her spasming cunt sank her pussy down along his erection and the head pushed inside her. "It's going in me Dominic," Priya moaned, not certain if she was cautioning him to pull out or simply expressing a reality.

The black Hercules was mauling both her bosoms together and kneading both her nipples. He was more expert than her husband making Priya lose her mind with wild lust. Dominic ceased his ministrations for a moment and said, "You're so hot and wet!" He gazed at her in wonder. "I had no clue." He clasped his lips back over a nipple and sucked hard, kneaded hard with his teeth almost to the point of chewing, crushing her bosom simultaneously.

Priya whimpered, her desire growing. She was humping up and down on the Herculean erection. "I can't control myself," Priya thought in dismay. Her pussy worked it way deeper. Dominic already felt enormous compared to her Indian husband. But, when his gigantic shaft pushed further than Navin's little penis had ever been, unknown pleasure zones inside her pussy stirred to greater heights. Dominic pulled his mouth off her tits long enough to turn upward and groan. That was the moment the

Indian wife lost control and lusted in absolute desire for the Black hunk. She grabbed his head and pulled his lips against hers. His tongue pushed into her mouth and her tongue pushed back. "I need more," she thoroughly considered bouncing over his erection wildly, "MORE!"

Priya raised back. "This is so wrong," she moaned. Her married Indian pussy no longer belonged only to her husband. She couldn't stop herself. She burned to feel Dominic's big black cock covered in her pussy. "Let's see how much I can take in," she moaned.

"Indeed! But once you go black, there is no going back," Dominic teased, not arguing. This was out of this world and a very pleasurable experience for the two of them.

Priya felt as if she was losing her virginity once more. Priya pushed back on his chest and looked deeply into his eyes as she gradually plunked down on his lap. "Good god," Dominic panted feeling the entirety of his big black cock covered in her warmth and wetness.

"Goodness Dominic, you're all in me," Priya moaned with some disbelief. Priya had never felt anything so great. The immense cock head felt like it had pushed into her belly and she could sense it shooting precum inside her. She couldn't move. Priya just sat on him, trembling and shaking. Her vaginal muscles were pressing and twitching all over his thick erection. "I'm

going to cum once more." She focused on the advancing and intense climax. It was growing in power, her pussy muscles shuddered over every last trace of his mammoth black pole.

"Your hot pussy's draining my cock, bitch," Dominic snorted. His hips were kicking as though he was desperate for her movements. "Going to cum!" he moaned.

That smashed her to reality. "Crap!" her eyes flew open. The pending climax blurred as her dread overwhelmed what was practically imminent. "Not in me. Pull out so I can put a condom on it." Priya screamed. The black Hercules didn't move and Priya acknowledged she was the one holding his mammoth shaft inside her. She propelled herself up, missing his erection when it dropped out of her.

Concealed Games – Part 4

Priya leaned over to the table beside the couch and opened it, searching for one of Navin's condoms. Dominic kneeled watching her, his erection stayed straight up, bigger now than when she'd seen it before. He'd been so close to ejaculating in her.

Priya opened the packet and pulled out the condom. She needed him back inside her as soon as possible which made her hands shake as she fumbled with the rubber. Dominic sat back on his knees, pushing his erection up and out. She hesitated with the condom close to the fat knob, looking again in wonder at the sheer size of the dark Herculean dick. The tremendous balls were spread out underneath it. She was approaching her fertile time and if those colossal nuts had blasted their seed inside her... well, she didn't even want to think about it.

Priya giggled wickedly as she rolled the condom down Dominic's penis. "They're so loose on Navin," she let him know. She tried to extend it further down his penis, yet the thing seemed to be stretched out to completely just to cover the head and the tip looked too small to hold all his discharge. "On your huge penis, it's hardly a shower cap." Priya laughed this time and lay down on her back spreading her legs for him.

Dominic climbed over her and it was Priya who guided his black pole back in. She grabbed the pole under the head and the condom, holding her labia open with her other hand as she guided his shaft down the passageway into her juicy pussy. Dominic lay down on her, grabbing her bosoms as he brought his weight down to push himself into her body.

This time he started the kiss and it was as enthusiastic as the first. Both the wife and black Hercules were equally loaded up with desire for each other's body and communicating it with their mouths.

Dominic worked his mammoth shaft in her, bucking his hips. After for a little while, he leaned over her, fucking her faster with her legs spread around his hips. All the time Priya made love with her pin-dick Indian husband, she faked most of her orgasms even screaming like a porn star on the urges of her husband. But this night was different. This time of her own will, Priya started talking like a porn star. "Fuck me! Fuck ME!" Priya screamed in stimulating ecstasy. "Give me that big black cock. Fuck this married Indian cunt harder!"

"Your hot pussy feels so great around my cock, bitch. I'm now the owner of this pussy," Dominic snorted.

"Oh! YES, Dominic, you are. Fuck me, Dominic, I love your huge cock." She clutched the cloth of the couch as her approaching climax developed. "FUCK! So great! So big!" Her hips bucked up

into each intense thrust of his mammoth black pole fucking him back as fast as he was slamming into her. "You're so much better than Navin," Priya moaned.

"Am I better?" Dominic inquired.

"Much fucking better," she snorted.

Dominic smiled from ear to ear once more. "You like this black cock better than Navin's?"

Priya felt guilt and wished she hadn't said it now; however, it was honest. "Your big black cock is far better than my pin-dick Indian husband. I love your enormous cock. I adore fucking your big black cock. Fuck ME!"

Fully inserted, Dominic's cock seemed to push up past her ribs towards her chest. Priya was shocked now, but Navin concentrating on his wife's moans from the guest room could sense how she loved it. Navin's pretty Indian wife was no longer his. He could never please her like Dominic. He couldn't compete with the black superiority and his massive shaft. There was more of him out than Navin had altogether. Priya would never be able to feel her cuck hubby's pathetic pin dick now anyway, after being stretched by a real man fucking her.

"Indeed, slut!" Dominic threw back his head, grabbing her knees in his solid arms. He raised her ass off the couch and hammered

his cock deeper. His face teethed as he slammed harder, faster and more brutishly. He howled, "CUMMING!"

"CUMMING!" Priya shouted as one. Priya's pussy spasm and then exploded around his cock as the greatest climax of her life shook her body. She could feel Dominic's cock kicking into her as he came, the head struck her cervix. Nothing in her life had ever felt so good...." OW!" Priya cried as the ecstatic delight transformed into torture. "Pull it out Dominic," Priya shouted in desperation as the agony became unendurable.

"But I'm not finished cumming," Dominic begged, in amazement, feeling his balls depleting.

"It hurts, pull it out. Please pull IT OUT NOW!" Priya grimaced, her face in torment and Dominic looked frightened as he yanked his mammoth throbbing erection back. She hadn't felt so much agony in her life. His whole cock hurt as it pulled out and when his enormous cockerel jumped up free, Priya realized why.

The condom was hardly sticking to Dominic's cock head. Not just the elastic, but nearly the whole of the condom was filled like a water balloon. Priya watched in wonderment as his big black cock kept on throbbing, jerking, and the condom kept on swelling even bigger. It was nearly as large as a newborn infant's head. "No big surprise why it hurt," Priya stated, bewildered as she hauled the straining condom still swinging from the tip of his erection. She gazed in sheer wonder while the rim of the

condom gradually slid off the head. She squeezed the lip just as it tumbled off his enormous shaft and held it up, gazing at the protruding sack. "That's a hell of a treat," Priya stated, gazing at the swelled-out rubber. Navin's seed only filled the nipple. Dominic's seed filled the whole condom. "Next time bring condoms that fit your size," she stated, swinging the substantial sperm filled ball before her face before tying it close.

Dominic was pulling his shorts up. He turned his head in astonishment. "Next time?"

Priya stood and the now dressed Dominic took her in his arms, grabbing her bosom. She remained on tiptoes and looked him in the eyes. "My husband will soon be out on business trip," she said with a saucy grin. "We can do this the whole time he's gone."

"We can fuck for days?"

"I'll need that big black dick in me the whole time he's gone," Priya replied and Dominic pulled her lips against his, kissing her more passionately than her husband ever had. She melted in his arms like wax in the fire and pressed her groin against his. She felt his erection gaining life under his shorts. Reluctantly, Priya pushed him away. "You need to go."

"I love you," Dominic stated, as a matter of fact.

"NO!" Priya asserted too rapidly. He had astonished her. However, she ought to have anticipated it. "This is simply sex. Incredible sex," she consoled him. "Yes, this is just awesome sex. Save your love for someone else."

"Truly, Priya," Dominic answered. Priya relaxed, down on the couch as Dominic gazed at her, shaking his head at her seductive lush body before turning for the door.

"Oh! Dominic," Priya stated, raising her hand. He paused for a moment. "When you get the condoms next time, purchase a value pack." Priya winked.

"Sure, Priya," Dominic acknowledged. He left the room and she heard his long strides bouncing down the stairs.

Priya turned and tossed the condom in her grasp. It was so heavy and provoked by her wild desire. She just wanted to hurl it against the wall like a water balloon. She raised it up to her head by the tied end and her black eyes gazed at the potent serum. She let it swing forward and backward like a heavy sack. She didn't have a clue why the sperm filled rubber entranced her so much. His semen was pure white, thicker than pudding, and had tasted so rich. "Thank god this thing held," Priya thought. "So much cum." Priya brought down the condom and slid up the couch, propping her back against the cushion. "So much cum." Priya loosened the knot at the end of the elastic. "So much cum," Priya exclaimed a third time, spilling its contents all over her

bosoms. "So much cum," she murmured, watching it splatter all over her luscious breasts. "What's happening to me?" Priya groaned. "Cum on me Dominic," she murmured, wanting him to still be here. The sperm was still warm, she thought. The enormous volume or the elastic sack had kept its heat.

A huge stream of white serum ran down her belly to pool in her navel. Priya ran her hand through it and rubbed Dominic's seed into her belly. Her other hand massaged it over her nipples. Aches of delight shook her body as she rubbed and squeezed her nipples.

Her body had come to life from her experience with the youthful black man. Priya wished he was here to fuck her once more. "OH! god Dominic, CUM ON ME!" The hand on her belly gathered up a wad of sperm and brought it up to her mouth. She licked his seed off her fingers disillusioned by the slight taste of latex and wanting to be licking it off his big black cock once more.

"Cum in my mouth," Priya wondered, licking her fingers clean. Her right hand pushed his semen down her belly and over the dainty portion of pubic hair. Her sticky fingers penetrated inside her pussy. "Cum in my pussy," she thought, shoving her fingers. She laid back, fingering herself faster, scooping and bringing a greater amount of his cum up to her mouth to suck. "CUMMING

FOR YOU Dominic!" she screamed as her fingers and her fantasy brought her off once more.

When Priya walked into the guest room, Navin pretended to be asleep. She had a bed sheet wrapped around her juicy tits. Priya sat beside Navin and began playing with his hair. After she touched him for some time, Navin pretended to wake up.

Priya said tenderly, "Hey sleepy head..."

Navin opened his eyes... looked at her while a courteous smile flickered on his lips... Priya grinned back and reached out for her hubby's pin dick. Clearly, it was hard... it was leaking.

"How was it, sweetheart?" Navin asked passionately.

Priya's eyes lit up, "It was fantastic. Thank you so much, hon! You are the best husband on the entire planet. I don't have the faintest idea of what I did to deserve you."

Priya continued playing with Navin and her hands were all over him. The material she had wrapped herself with loosened and tumbled off. Navin now had a reasonable view of the aftermath. There was cum all over her face and hair and streamed down her breasts. Her hair was all messy. Her nipples were swollen and somewhat purple. She came nearer to Navin and he could smell the sex on her body. She came closer and gave him a passionate kiss.

Priya murmured, "So did you enjoy watching your wife fuck a real stud?"

Before Navin could respond, she gestured and kept on stroking him. Navin's yearning eyes followed the indications and all of a sudden, he began to tremble as he saw the bite marks on her breasts.

"This...this," he was shaking.

"He has left his mark on me," Priya answered passionately and moved her clenched hand quicker on his pin dick, "Kiss it, this is for you."

Navin shivered as he put his lips on her boobs and began to splash his cum over her hands. Right then and there the power was back.

For Priya nothing was as in the past; she was on edge not knowing how Navin would take her consensual adultery. Yet, she felt empowered and independent. She was already financially independent since she had a secure job as a Sales and Marketing Assistant in the reputed advertising firm. And now when she had the independence of engaging in a sexual relationship outside her marriage with her husband's consent, she felt sexually independent. Not too many women enjoyed that exquisite luxury or unrestricted freedom. Priya started the entire whole thing with the idea to just tease Navin and give him

a taste of his fantasy. But she got so psychologically involved in it that she couldn't resist the forbidden temptation.

The first time alone with Navin after that night, she discovered that he was, in reality, a cuckold; she could see it all over his face. It was confirmed when Navin became overly obsessed with her succulent tits which bore Dominic's teeth marks. Not only did he kissed those marks, but he also experienced an explosive orgasm while kissing those spots. When they had a brainstorming discussion about her experience and wishes on his birthday, Priya was relieved to discover that Navin was upbeat and understood that he was experiencing every feeling of a genuine, loving cuckold. Priya had a magnificent encounter and immensely satisfying experience. She finally realized that it would be hard for her to forget it.

Priya couldn't help comparing the two indispensable men in her life. On one side was her better half, Navin, whom she loved so much and who was so caring, loving and admiring towards her that he would never confine her in any cage. Then there was this Herculean hunk Dominic, who drew out the crude desire, the raw lust in her; the true feelings which she had perhaps buried in the deep corners of her mind.

Priya felt loved and cared for her better half; but ached for the hard touch of a man; a man who could fuck her with bestial wrath and use her body for his pleasure.

As for Navin, he couldn't believe his luck at how his deviant fantasies got fulfilled. Although he got tremendously excited watching his wife get impaled on a mammoth big black cock, somewhere in the corners of his perverted mind he felt insecure. Jealousy reared its ugly head when he realized he wasn't able to provide the stimulating pleasures of the highest heaven to his legally wedded wife.

Insecurities vanquished his moral feelings when his twisted mind faced the brutal question of what if his wife left him for Dominic. The jealousy and insecurity were so overpowering for Navin that he practically had to leave the cuckolding session in progress and retreat to the guest bedroom to spend the rest of the night. His mind raced from one thought to another never allowing him to calm his excitement and to sleep.

But, then again, a peculiar enthusiasm pricked his twisted soul and affirmed that he was experiencing the most blissful stage of his life by being a fortunate cuckold, by allowing his wife to be in the arms of another man who could easily fuck her brains out.

After nearly two weeks, the matter popped up in their bedroom once again.

Priya grabbed Navin's hairs and groaned softly as he licked her pussy, "Yesss... that's it, baby..."

Navin moved his tongue between the pussy lips and lapped enthusiastically, feeling her growing excitement. As a matter of fact, he was also enthusiastically stirred beyond limits as they were in the sixty-nine position. Priya was delicately licking and stroking his hard erection.

"Was he rough with you," Navin murmured in a dry voice, slightly lifting his head from her groin.

"Don't stop..." Priya pushed back his head as she was lying beneath him.

"Yes... he was..." Priya flicked her tongue over his hardened pole. "He took me very forcefully and I loved that," she asserted stirring him further.

Navin realized this wsn't some made up story from her. This had really happened right in front of him. He saw her ecstatic hip movements on Dominic's mammoth black pole, heard her uproarious groans and cries while Dominic fucked her; moans that he as her husband wouldn't be able to make her do. He began to eat her with extraordinary vigor showering his oral tributes on her rosebuds while Priya stroked and licked his erection with the most extreme consideration to drag out the ecstatic pleasure as much as possible. Navin caressed her bubble butts and drove his tongue further into her moistening pussy and asked her to take him into her mouth.

The entire scene flashed back in his mind, how until the last moment he was absolutely unsure whether Priya would just tease Dominic or would really do it with him.

He couldn't believe it when she undressed and played along. As Navin replayed the erotic, twisted scenes in his deviant mind, he realized he couldn't keep going longer and thrust forward his pin dick into her mouth. Priya too sensed her husband's urgency and quit teasing him and slurped in an enormous piece of the erection inside her hot mouth. Almost immediately he began to cum.

In the wake of having his pleasure, Navin earnestly concentrated on pleasuring his wife as she held his head with both hands and guided him. Priya shut her eyes and relished in the euphoric excitement, yearning for the strong hands of Dominic on her body, his mouth on her succulent bosoms, brutally mauling, pinching and kneading her assets. She grabbed one hand of Navin's and placed it over her boobs and groaned.

"Harder..." Priya moaned, "take me...ugggg..." She kicked her crotch and shuddered into a hard climax.

"You know Dominic called today. We were online for a long time." Priya stated after they were done pleasuring each other orally and lay panting.

"What does he want now?" Navin was extra attentive.

"Well, you know. He's in Seattle handling a lucrative deal. He just called to check about the advertisement paperwork," Priya sighed. "But, yes. He sounded excited and asked me to continue from where we left," she put her head on his chest.

"What did you say?" Navin's heart pounded a thousand times faster.

"Of course, I won't," she replied instantly, "However, I hope you realize I feel terrible. I have led him into this."

Priya hugged Navin tightly and continued, "He felt that I was in a terrible marriage with you." She sighed and continued again, "That's why it all happened and he was insisting that we should meet. He was not ready to understand why I was saying no... so I told him the truth."

"What?!" Navin was shocked, "You let him know everything?"

"Yes obviously, I needed to make him understand that all was well and will be well among us. That I am content with my husband... He understood at last and was chuckling at himself, at his sheer luck to be tricked so easily."

"Oh!" Navin breathed.

"So what do you say, should we meet him?" Priya sounded serious.

Navin felt a thousand bass drums pounding in his heart as he understood that his wife was requesting to be with another man. He cuddled nearer to her and kissed her delicately on her luscious lips.

"I don't have the faintest idea. What do you think?" His voice was more like a pleading than an inquiry.

"I never imagined that I could ever do it. But it happened... In addition, I believed that you would never let it happen in reality in spite of the fact that you were constantly amped up for it... I thought you would always let it remain as a twisted and wild fantasy of yours. But you did... and also, you are quite cool about it," Priya talked slowly but intently, stroking his hairs. "Now, Dominic is insisting for it again... He says for one last time."

Navin was trembling in excitement as he heard her out, "Would you like to do it?" It seemed Navin was almost choking with fervor.

"Well, I think one final time won't hurt, will it? Obviously, only if you approve," she murmured with equal excitement. Navin was not deaf and dumb to his wife's emotions.

He felt an ache of envy; meeting the man who had fucked his wife's brains out, was never his wildest dream. But the idea that she needed another man to pleasure and please her stimulated his excitement. The fact that his wife had fallen for a far more

potent man than him stirred him beyond limits and soon his floppy pin dick twitched with earnestness. The thrills from the fact that his better half was ecstatically pleased by a man were all that he thought about. In his deviant fantasies, the other man never had a face or a body like Dominic's; it was just sex, wild sex. However, at this point, Dominic was a real man about whom his wife spoke. Everything that happened or would happen would without a doubt be what she'd loved and would love more.

Whenever Navin was sleeping with his wife the 'other man' had been just between them to stir up their passionate stimulations; not physically present, but in their role-play. It drove him insane and he essentially couldn't get Priya's animated statement out of his mind, "He has left his mark on me." This was his most earnestly desired twisted fantasy. His educated modern yet traditional Indian wife with high moral values was corrupted and taken by a potent man right in front of him while he watched.

Although he couldn't continue watching the last time and left in the middle, he was sure to crack the nut this time. He couldn't forget the desire, the cravings, the wild lust when she melted like wax in Dominic's embrace. He kissed her all over her body emptying his passion. Navin was subconsciously being protective towards Priya as though she was some valuable

possession, which was on the verge of being snatched away by a foreign invader.

Although Priya promised Navin that what happened between her and Dominic and was just a one-time affair and would never happen again, her determination crumbled when Dominic called her. Her perverted mind reminded her how intensely erotic the experience was and she figured out how to slow him down.

In any case, two weeks passed and she was thinking about giving the desire a chance to manage her rather than her mind, 'one final time and after that never again, she would be a good wife again.'

So it was fixed and Saturday night they were meeting Dominic at his home for supper. Dominic was back from Seattle and was dying to hold Priya in his arms. Priya too was keen to meet him after almost three weeks and fly the highest heavens of pleasure. Priya came out of the shower wrapped in a towel, water dripping from her wet hair. She grinned and sat before the dresser drying her long-wet hair. Regardless of how frequently Navin had seen her like this, it still never failed to stimulate his arousal. She unknotted the towel and grabbed yellow panties from the dresser. Navin watched her slip into the tiny piece of silken fabric, bringing it up over her buxom buttocks. The panties looked much smaller compared to her tempting curves and seductive lush body, only two triangles: one in the front and one

in the back. The front triangle was hardly able to conceal the prized rosebuds; so puffy and swollen yearning to be tribute to potent juices. Navin was hypnotized watching the swollen mound desperately trying to hide behind the tight fitting fabric.

Concealed Games – Part 5

"Enjoying what you're seeing?" Priya said as she blushed. "Go out and wait for me," she affectionately rebuked him and he reluctantly strolled to the living room.

Navin settled down on a couch, where his mom, dad, and his distant relative Jagan were watching the auditions of America's Got Talent.

Navin's mom Maya was 46 years old, still very youthful and jubilant in spirit. Navin's father Deblal was 66, with health issues. Jagan Murugan was 55 and Deblal's brother and very close family companion. Twenty years back when Deblal was struggling to settle in the USA, Jagan helped Deblal and Maya with all his resources.

"Amazing!! What a singer," Maya suddenly exclaimed in excitement at the TV. Navin snapped out of his trance and hastily gazed at the TV.

"Where had you gone son?" she asked, "You never miss live auditions of AGT."

"I was just thinking about a website design plan. I can always watch the repeat telecasts," Navin pointed at the repeat telecast of the show flashing in the corner of the screen.

"Since when did you start thinking about work at home," his dad stared at him in amusement.

All of them laughed out loud at Deblal's hilarious comments including Priya who had just walked into the living room and heard what her father-in-law had said.

Navin realized it was all in good fun and he too laughed at his dad's sense of humor. He glanced at his better half and discovered her as the same loving and caring wife; responsible and kind-hearted daughter-in-law taking care of the family whenever the in-laws visited.

However, his mind was troubled by the fact that she was the same woman who, at night, fulfilled his deviant fantasies and the one who was prepared to go with him to meet her black lover.

"Wow bahu!! You look extraordinary, so sexy," Maya yelled enthusiastically upon seeing Priya as she came out of the bedroom wearing her new sleeveless and backless sari; a blue one this time. (Bahu is the Indian name of daughter-in-law)

The backless design highlighted her lush back and showed she wasn't wearing a bra. Priya grinned at her youthful mom-in-law's lovely compliment,

"Thanks, mom. You had better be in bed early because tomorrow morning you three need to attend the charity

135

function," she told them. Maya made a face. "That's my bahu. Always keeping the family in line," acknowledged Jagan. Deblal, Maya, and Jagan were in the management body of a charitable trust taking care of underprivileged children and helping them in their higher studies and healthcare.

Maya although in her mid-forties, never showed any signs of aging neither in her face nor in her spirit. In fact, with every passing year, her glamour and elegance increased her God made beauty.

Unlike Priya, she was a more or less authoritarian in Navin's family being his mother. She maintained a strict glamorous lifestyle and, as a hardcore feminist, always believed in female independence. Her buxom bottom and perky chest mounds were enough to turn any man's head even in her mid-forties.

Maya realized her son Navin and bahu Maya wouldn't be back until morning as her bahu had already told her that if Navin got too drunk, she wouldn't drive home late at night.

Navin was an occasional drinker; only at parties and gatherings. Priya never told her mom-in-law what party they were going to attend. Maya grinned as she realized that the house would be hers for tonight; her husband had heart problems and would soon retire to his bedroom as he had already taken his dinner and pills; and the maidservant would leave around 8:00 PM. She planned to sleep with her sweetheart Jagan in his room

tonight. Yes, that was true. Maya and Jagan had been physical from the time she and Deblal had arrived in the US. "Nothing comes free in this world," was Jagan's assertion and Maya accepted his proposal allowing her husband to get a lucrative job and settle down in Los Angeles. However, unlike Priya who was mindful about Navin's feelings, Maya had been cheating on Deblal with Jagan for nearly twenty years now. In fact, Maya was somewhat bewildered when it came to her loving relationship with Deblal and physical relationship with Jagan.

As time passed, she was so confused with her relationship status that she'd decided to end her relationship with Deblal. But Deblal had a serious accident and Navin was too young as a five-year-old to take care of his dad and family. So, plans changed. Since then, she had been physical with Jagan. Jagan never married because he was her de facto husband.

Navin drove the Jaguar and every now and again glanced at his ravishing wife seated next to him. Priya pushed back her long hair and kept looking forward at the passing city lights and night sight.

Navin was battling the urge to turn the car around and return home to protect his most prized possession while Priya was torn into pieces between the feelings of wild lust for Dominic and her passionate love for Navin. She was unable to look at her husband or utter a single word. The cold breeze from the car's

air conditioning raised goosebumps on her glowing skin and made chills flow down her spine. They reached Dominic's residence at 7:30, as planned.

"Hello!" Dominic welcomed them at the door. He was grinning and held out his hand to Navin. Navin warmly greeted Dominic murmuring something of a welcome as they went inside. But that chuckle, that grin had a faint touch of embarrasment and Navin's heart skipped a beat when he realized Dominic's tone.

They were shown into an enormous and luxurious living and dining room area and settled themselves on the couch. Navin fidgeted anxiously not understanding what to say under such uncomfortable circumstances. He felt too intimidated to speak. He glanced at his wife from the corner of his eye for help yet discovered none. She too was a little uncomfortable as a result of her own conflicts and blushed taking time to look around at the neatly decorated room.

"Wow man!! You're simply great," Dominic suddenly addressed Navin, "You're one hell of a daredevil to do something like this," he concluded excitedly and Navin just returned the favor as he smiled sheepishly.

"That is a strikingly bold and daring step for both of you to transform your fantasies into realities," Dominic continued. "You really got me that night," he roared with laughter. The grin and giggling seemed, to be cordial and Navin relaxed as he could

discern no arrogant looks which stated, 'I am the man fucking your wife, mate.'

"It was not our aim to trick you," Priya clarified, "It was just instinctive," she talked reluctantly. As time progressed, Navin felt left out as Priya and Dominic continued to flirt and talk to each other.

Meanwhile, back at their home, Jagan arrived at the room where Maya was waiting for her lover. Maya blushed when Jagan stating, "How's my slut doing tonight?"

Maya was stupefied at Jagan's lecherous comment especially when her husband Deblal had just closed his eyes. Maya shushed and seductively twisted herself on the bed provoking Jagan's arousal. Deblal's once faithful wife Maya invited Jagan to sit beside her on the bed. The masculine stud was in a sleeveless, shirt exhibiting his enormous muscles.

Maya heart increased its beat. Her entire body shuddered with excitement when she recollected how this hunky man looked in the buff. Her significant other had a pleasant enough body for his age; however he was no muscular god like Jagan. As time passed, Maya allowed her wild lust to corrupt her and licked her lips seductively to further tempt Jagan. Her mind was flooded with sinful thoughts of how she was going to fly the highest peaks of lust with her lover.

Her line of reasoning was cut short when Jagan unexpectedly jumped on her and kissed her feverishly on her fleshy lips. Her first response was an absolute surprise, but soon she melted in his amorous embrace. He devoured her luscious lips with his thick lips. His tongue invaded her mouth, meeting her soft tongue, swapping saliva. So began this evening's sexual pleasures.

Dominic was a decent host and served drinks. Priya just drank sodas. Navin was upbeat as he needed a solid drink to calm his nerves. They had food and drinks and snacks which Dominic had ordered from a nearby restaurant and kept on talking; Navin was quite reserved.

Dominic figured out how to bring the point back over and over to the night he spent with Priya. He showered her with praises and recommendations like how strong she was, how independent and mature she was and how her qualities were a perfect blend to her seduction. Priya seemed to enjoy the flirts and compliments and started to open up more as the evening progressed. She even told him that he was her secret crush at the office, which made Dominic chuckle wickedly.

"It must be truly exciting for you," he suddenly addressed Navin, "So, do how you feel about being a cuckold for real?"

Navin was embarrassed by such a direct question and was not prepared for it. He looked at Priya who was blushing too. He

didn't have the faintest idea what to say as his face reddened in humiliation.

"It's extremely unfair for me," Navin finally said. "While you two were enjoying yourselves I was completely in the dark and just thinking about the stud that was able to seduce my better half." He talked in a tone as though he was the victim.

"Are you complaining?" Priya asked.

"How could I complain!" he grinned, "It was a night I would always remember," he moved next to Priya.

"Oh! Man! I think you walked away from the scene," Dominic snickered and continued, "Besides, you can always watch us. Can't he, dear?" He turned to Priya.

"I must confess I have never seen such an excellent, adventurous and brave lady," Dominic held Priya's hand as he moved beside her. Navin felt hurt as he was half expecting that Priya might push his hands away yet she didn't do anything.

"What am I thinking? This is the reason we're here. She is here to fuck him." Navin questioned inwardly as he discovered Priya gleaming in fervor and extremely glamorous. "But every last bit of her glamour is going to be ravished by this man." Navin breathed hard as jealousy spread through him. All he could do was to take a big gulp of his drink.

Jagan was a true lion as always ravishing Maya's lush body. His hands were all over her, squeezing her succulent bosoms with a force that drove her to the point of excruciating agony, pressing and slapping her juicy pussy. But then again, Maya loved the blend of pain and pleasure. She always yearned for her man to be rough and hard with her.

The pressure, the powerful sexual ministrations and the tempting imagination of his naked body on hers were a lot for her. In two minutes Maya was shivering in lecherous desire. She found herself topless; her brawny lover sucking voraciously at her perky nipples, kneading them, chewing them, licking them while his hands mauled her enormous bosoms.

Maya had never given anybody else the chance to ravage her like this. Her husband Deblal was so gentle on her unlike this bull ravishing her. Pushing at her nightgown, Jagan ordered the caring mother and cheating wife to take it off and soon the panties followed.

There she was, a married traditional Indian mother, absolutely stripped on the bed with a brawny stud, being sexually used by a man who wasn't her husband. Jagan was a specialist in dealing with married women and especially MILFs who had decent loving husbands like Deblal. He always knew how to liberate the whore inside them; the true woman that their decent, loving

husbands did not know even existed. That was the charisma by which he had been penetrating Maya behind her husband's back.

Taking his left hand, Jagan grabbed Maya's moistening pussy and started to play with it and press on it. A deep lustful groan escaped Maya's mouth. These were stimulating sensations that she had always experienced whenever she was with Jagan. Without notice, Maya felt one finger penetrating into her sacred chamber as one of her perky nipples was all the while being chomped, kneaded and sucked voraciously by Jagan.

She bounced in pleasurable excitement on the bed and snaked her hands on his huge muscular forearm desperately attempting to push it away. Instead, Jagan shoved his finger further into the cheating wife's pussy. Maya felt her juices streaming and she wasn't able to resist the brutal ministrations of her lover any further. She let him keep on fingering her.

Priya was feeling anxious as Dominic pulled her close and she looked towards Navin. She realized this was going to give him heartache; however, he needed to experience this agonizing suffering to accomplish what he was longing for. The real happiness of being a cuckold is in the agony to see your wife in passionate and desperate lust for another man and realizing that

she appreciates him using her for his masculine lust. Priya relaxed in Dominic's arms.

There was an uncomfortable and unusual silence in the room with the exception of the clamor of the AC system. Dominic caressed her delicate body in his arms passionately moving his palm over her hair, cheeks, and neck. Navin squirmed with his glass and made an effort not to look at them. He felt furious with Dominic for touching her so affectionately and sensually and with Priya for succumbing to his smooth traps.

"Why don't you just fuck my wife and be done with it?" his perverted mind screamed helplessly, "Just take out your enormous big black cock and shove it inside her pussy." Furthermore, he was extremely infuriated when Dominic turned her head and to put his mouth over her trembling juicy lips.

Navin watched in anguish as Dominic kissed her luscious lips and Priya's eyelids gradually shut and her mouth opened to kiss him back. Navin found it difficult to breathe as he watched their tongues meet and exchange saliva. He understood with a sickening dread that he had no power over this reality. Dominic wasn't simply going to put his mammoth cock inside her. He was going to explore Priya's entire body with amorous intent, in any way he was allowed to do. He wasn't simply going to fuck her. Rather, he was going to make her fall for him, crave him and finally conquer her lively spirit. One of Dominic's hands was

now on Priya's blouse and he was mauling her firm and ample tits with full force. Navin couldn't bear it any longer and nearly jumped up from his seat. The sound of his abrupt movement reached Priya and she opened her eyes only to find him standing in front of her, gazing intently.

"Are you OK, hon?" Priya was frightened.

Navin couldn't answer and he just poured himself another drink and stared away from them feeling helpless and humiliated. Priya understood that he was in agony. She squirmed out of Dominic's hold and rushed to Navin and embraced him firmly showering kisses all over his face.

"I love you, sweetie," Priya cooed a few times and kept on kissing Navin.

Dominic was outrageous that his fuck toy had slipped out of his grasp. He gritted his teeth, "You filthy perverted asshole... why does he have to interfere?" He was furious, unable to calm down at this unwanted intrusion. He wanted to kick Navin's ass out of the room.

Navin was amazed and so happy when he found that Priya was so worried about him. He was elated when he realize that Dominic was just her fuck toy and had no place in Priya's heart. He was the sole conqueror of her heart no matter the circumstances. In any case, his joy was brief as she held his

throbbing cock and chuckled, "You... you... you scared the shit out of me... you naughty boy."

"Sweetie, I know it's hard for you to watch," Priya stroked his hair and talked intently, "Why don't you just chill in the extra room?" Navin was disheartened; his heart skipped a beat at the heartbreaking proposal.

"I'll tell you everything in the morning," Priya murmured deviously and then winked.

"Morning!! She'd already made plans to spend the whole night with him," Navin didn't have a clue what to say. Dominic, who was listening to everything impatiently, moved in. He didn't want to relinquish this opportunity. He embraced Priya from behind jabbing his hardened erection against her ass.

"Why are you getting so restless?" Priya snickered while Dominic pulled her away from Navin. He turned her around and gripped her in his masculine arms like a hawk gripping its prey. Navin watched her as she squirmed and giggled in his arms.

Back at Navin's place, Navin's mother Maya was enjoying her ecstatic pleasure rides with her lover Jagan. Removing his pajama bottoms, Jagan remained in his messy shirt while being totally stripped from the waist down. Before he'd come to grab her, Jagan had removed his boxers. It was quicker this way.

Jagan sensed that the married cheating mother's cunt was well lubed from her own juices so he lifted her up in his masculine arms and let her down on his huge erect pole. When the precum covered cock head of the potent stud touched Maya's cunt lips, a jolt of electricity coupled with a chilling flow shot through her entire body from her toes to her head.

Moaning a little louder as she was brought down on Jagan's huge fuck pole, Maya felt her cunt being dilated. The first time she experienced such a wild feeling was when she brought forth her child, Navin. She had never experienced this feeling with her better half Deblal. Gradually, the Indian mother sunk on the big hardened erection until she was completely impaled on the masculine stud's monster. Maya clutched Jagan's broad shoulders as he impaled her on his hardened manhood.

She saw her wedding ring on her hand as the symbol of her faithfulness, trust, and commitment to her loving and caring husband Deblal. But right now, she wasn't thinking straight, all her thinking was focused on her cunt and on the mammoth pussy breaker conquering her worldly senses. As Maya raised and lowered her body on the potent shaft, her succulent bosoms jiggled and loud sultry groans escaped from her throat as if she were being exorcised. Maya shut her eyes as the delightful ecstasy of pain and pleasure in her overstretched cunt overwhelmed her.

"Is this how a woman should feel when she is filled to the brim with a masculine hunk's potent shaft?" Maya wondered in her own euphoric delight. "Why do I miss all these stimulating pleasures with Deblal and only experience them with Jagan?"

Maya's amorous mind was crowded with all sorts of illicit questions. She was unable to make decisions; but she knew one thing for sure: the lustful delights she was experiencing, was from another man, Jagan, her ardent lover of twenty years who made her sit on a cloud high above, each and every time.

Concealed Games – Part 6

Dominic was too desperate for Priya to delay the proceedings any further or to allow the married couple to reconsider their proposition. He immediately placed his mouth over her juicy lips and began to pull her sari. Priya wriggled feeling shy before her husband, yet Dominic figured out how to uncover her sexy thighs.

Navin watched the gradual and inevitable surrender of his better half into this Black Hercules's muscular arms and the torment gradually transformed into a shivering sensation. He truly wanted his wife to make the most out of her ecstatic time with her lover and was no longer agitated. Dominic raised her sari further and exposed the yellow panties, the tiny silken fabric scarcely covering her swollen sacred hole. His firm hands spread her smooth thighs further apart and squeezed the velvety pussy mounds causing Priya to moan.

"Isn't she hot... would you please take her panties off for me," Dominic asked Navin taking control of the proceedings. But his voice had more of a commanding tone than that of a request.

Undressing his wife for a black man to fuck, was so humiliating for Navin; but, the idea itself sent chills of lewd sensation through his spine twitching his pin dick and making it leak with excitement. He saw his wife look at him eagerly. He stood,

uncertain for a minute and then gradually proceeded to follow the orders of the man of the hour.

"Hold the sari and don't give it a chance to fall back," Dominic asked Priya who quietly agreed.

Navin stooped before his wife slipped off the fine fabric revealing a well-moistened vagina. Jets of thin pleasure juices had flowed down her inner thighs as a proof of her own sensual stimulations. Navin was so close that he could inhale the aroma of her excitement and he continued kneeling before her almost hypnotized by the excellence of the freshly shaved pussy.

"Much appreciated, cuck," Dominic asserted, "Now you can rest here while I take your wife to my bedroom. Obviously, it's better if you leave us alone and allow us to make the most out of it just like the other night... she would not enjoy your presence."

Navin wanted to watch Dominic fuck his wife this time. He was desperate to watch his mammoth big black cock sliding all through his wife's married Indian pussy. He was dying to devour the sight of the black stud cracking his nuts in his wife's sacred spot. But he couldn't speak a word as Dominic slowly escorted her to his room. Navin felt so alone, so abandoned as the door was slammed in his face.

Priya relaxed once she was alone with her lover, Dominic. She felt inhibited in front of her husband. Dominic pulled her to the

bed and she traced the layout of his hardened erection through his pants. She'd been eagerly waiting for this moment for the last few weeks. She eagerly pulled his pants down and impatiently dragged down his boxers. She breathed heavily as soon as the big black mamba waiting for its Indian pit throbbed in front of her face. Her eyes gleamed in sensual wonderment. Seeing his gigantic black torpedo dancing in front of her, Priya felt her pussy catch fire. She took his mammoth black cock in her warm mouth and sucked it for a few moments. The musky aroma of the potent shaft was enough to make her juices leak.

Dominic pushed her on the bed and moved over her, squeezing and mauling her succulent bosoms firmly. Priya breathed out heavily, gasping for air at his hard touch and promptly the desire took over as she saw the desire in his eyes.

Chills gushed down her spine making her shudder like a leaf in a whirlwind. She felt the difference between raw, passionate lust of the Black Hercules using her as a sex toy, and the delicate lovemaking of her husband. Her mind was crowded with corrupt thoughts as Dominic took control of her body.

"My husband is in the other room. Make me scream your name out for him," Priya chuckled deviously. Without further ado, he raised her legs high and wide and thrust himself right in her flooding married pussy.

"Ahhh...Good God!" she tossed her head back in the wild ecstasy.

He began to pound her pussy hard. Priya lay with her legs wrapped around his waist getting a charge out of each thrust. Dominic was in no rush and he fucked her harder and fucked her long.

Priya appreciated surrendering herself completely to his animalistic thrusts and came twice in quick succession which she didn't recall doing in a long time.

Navin was gazing blankly at the closed door of the room. He was shaking with undefined feelings, something which he had never experienced before as he heard the hard slamming of Dominic's erection into his wife's womanhood. His pin dick oozed juices and was agonizingly hard for a long time and he adjusted it before settling down on the couch again.

He made himself another drink and took the glass to his parched lips with shaking hands. Sitting alone allowed him a chance to think about what he had done. He had brought his wife to her lover so that they could enjoy mind-blowing fucking. He had never seen his wife so excited and he felt joy, realizing that the Black Hercules was fucking her brains out. Her gorgeous, lush body would be violated by a potent stud.

Navin was on a sexual high and he didn't want to jerk off as he didn't want to come down from that high. He realized this wouldn't be the last time. There would be many more occasions like this. The sound of the bed rocking sent chills gushing down his spine as the muscular virile stud performed his lustful duties.

Navin heard his wife Priya screaming. Yes! Priya was screaming as her legs were up high up in the air and the big black cock was pistoning all through her married pussy. She begged the Black Hercules to fuck her hard, to stuff her with his big black cock. She told him she worshipped him. She loved him more than her husband of 3 years when it came down to raw passion. Dominic on the other hand, made Priya scream out his name and asserted to whom those married holes belonged. A great many orgasms shook her body as Dominic mauled her juicy bosoms and fucked her flooding cunt for his pleasure. Their lips intertwined often as though they were a married couple performing their duty in their bed. It was just that the cuckold husband was supplanted by a more potent male.

The fucking lasted several hours this time. The sheets reeked of cum and vaginal liquids as Dominic exhausted his overwhelming saggy balls inside the Indian wife's womb multiple times.

After the exceptional sex, they lay depleted in one another's arms. Priya felt remorseful as she realized that she was doing this not for her better half's fantasy, but rather for her own sexual satisfaction.

She was frightened as she nestled with Dominic, she would not like to build up any affection for him apart from the raw animalistic sex. However, she couldn't resist her feelings and exquisitely relished being enveloped in his masculine arms. Priya kissed Dominic on his smooth chest feeling the afterglow of sex and realized he would be hard soon. He prodded her to keep kissing him and pushed her head lower on his waist. Priya knew what he wanted.

Priya slipped lower kissing and licking his body and stroking the flaccid pole. With her lustful eyes, she looked at him before taking him in her mouth.

"Ahhh...," Dominic groaned as the hot mouth engulfed his cock head. He felt control over this delightful lady who was extending her pretty lipstick decorated lips around his big black cock. He set a hand on the back of her head and slipped his cock deeper in her mouth. The cock immediately extended to its most extreme and expanded her mouth. Priya realized that what she was doing was way past the honorable obligation of an adoring wife; however, felt an unreasonable joy and a perverse pleasure,

forgetting about every thought as she devoured and slurped on to the thick black mamba.

In her bedroom, Maya felt the electrifying delight, she was given by Jagan's 8-inch fuck pole. Even if she added up all the love nights with her husband in twenty-seven years of her marriage, her husband Deblal was no match for this potent hunk who always drove her insane and gave her wings to fly the ecstatic pleasures of the highest heavens.

Suddenly, Jagan grabbed Maya by her waist and she watched his muscles flexing as he moved her faster up and down on his throbbing erection. If anybody had ventured into the room discreetly, they would definitely consider Maya to be a whore pleasuring the potent stud in the bedroom. But Maya didn't care. Her world was Jagan, vigorously shoving his potent shaft in her married pussy and using her as a fuck toy. Her lustful moans became more intense and Maya muffled herself with her hand not to awaken her cuck husband Deblal sleeping in the other room, as Jagan's gigantic erection filled her totally.

"I'm going to fuck your daughter-in-law slut. I'm going to make her my whore too." Jagan breathed in Maya's ears, sending chills of ecstasy down her spine.

"Please don't do that," Maya's voice was husky. "She is my son's wife."

"She is a slut waiting to be freed just like you!" Jagan groaned.

To add to all this, Jagan started biting feverishly at the Indian mother's huge milk buckets. He was completely consumed by his overpowering lust for this fuck toy. What's more, whenever the thought of the pimp cuckold husband, Deblal, crossed his mind, his manhood throbbed harder. He was passionately aroused by the act of taking his brother's most prized possession, his wife Maya.

After 45 minutes of riding the gigantic erection, Maya was delirious; she had already climaxed multiple times and the stud under her was still continuing fucking her brains out.

Looking into his eyes, Maya discovered an animalistic lust as Jagan gritted his teeth bellowed. Soon she felt the cock head of the shaft ramming her womanhood expand and the balls boiling under her married pussy. Stream after stream of intense hot cum burned her womb and cervix. She yelled at the electrifying sensation shuddering as her hands were unable to muffle her cries. Jagan violated her juicy lips kissing her in lust while she kissed him back in gratitude for the amorous delight, he had given her.

After they finished, surges of white cum spilled out of the Indian mother's freshly fucked womanhood as her bosoms were marked with love bites from the potent stud.

The first light of the morning began to pour in from the open window and Priya got up stretching her arms. She breathed in the fresh air of the morning as her mind crowded with the illicit adventures of the previous night. She looked around and saw she was still in bed with Dominic, who was resting oblivious to world. She rapidly got up and pulled his shirt over her naked body and opened the door. Navin was sleeping on the couch, but likely not as well as he would have in his own bed.

Priya sat beside him and caressed his hair. Navin gradually opened his eyes and saw his gorgeous wife beside him. Her hair was disheveled and she was wearing a baggy shirt. He understood whose shirt it was and where from she was coming. Moreover, her cheeks, neck, and lips bore the love bites of her ardent lover. Priya kissed him on the forehead and greeted him, "Good morning love! I love you so much."

"I love you too sweetheart. Please let's go home now," Navin literally begged as he embraced her in his warmth.

"Yes, my love! Let's go home!" Priya kissed his lips and acknowledged.

Sex Story 5: Blood of Emotions

Until the minute my stepfather strolled into the casino, I had led a really typical life. I was raised mostly by my mom. My stepfather hadn't come into the picture until I was about to go to college. Our relationship was pretty typical. However, I had a bit of a secret crush on him, and I was happy that I'd moved out before he'd come to know of it.

It had been a very long time since he and I had talked. However, he remembered me quickly as he ventured into the poker room.

"Howdy, Chelsea," he said, sitting next to me at the table. From the beginning I felt a surge of panic that he was going to tell my mother I was out at a gambling club. But, I was 26 and making a truly decent career at playing cards, so I doubted anybody would mind.

"Hey, Daddy." It felt peculiar to call a man in his mid-forties 'Daddy' when I was in my mid-twenties. But that's what I'd always called him.

"What are you doing in Vegas?" He and my mom spent their time and energy living a boring life in Wisconsin.

"I came here to attend a bachelor party for one of my friends." He exclaimed boisterous, exceptionally drunk.

"Are you playing professionally now?" he inquired, and I grinned.

"That doesn't surprise me in the least. You always were three steps ahead of everyone else." He tapped my head warmly, and I faked a snarl at my mussed hair.

Daddy giggled and pulled out a rack of chips to be entered into the game.

"Hold up there, Daddy. I would prefer not to take your cash." It was my chance to prod him, and I was having a ton of fun with it.

"It's alright, darling. Your dad's not actually a sucker at the table." He smiled and gazed at the cards he'd been dealt before wagering an enormous pile of chips.

I glanced down at the cards I was holding. Two Aces. You're in for it now, Daddy. "Raise. To...three-fifty." I added three $100 chips to the bet, sending the challenge back to him.

"I'm all in." I scarcely gave him an opportunity to get his chips into the center of the table before I called his bet, triumphantly flipping my cards. He snickered and showed the table his hand, containing the other two aces. The hand was a draw, and we both withdrew our bets.

"I've gotta run, darling. It was great to see you. We should play some more while I'm in town." He brought forth his wallet and took two cards, giving them both to me. The main one contained his personal data, including his telephone number, occupation (dermatologist and skin specialist), and email address. The second was a hotel key. He winked as I gazed at it.

"I'm in my own room. Come up today around evening time if you're interested in a private game." Taking one of my hands in his, he pressed firmly before letting it go.

Without another word, he hurried off to join his friends who'd just arrived, hollering alongside them as they tore apart the Las Vegas Strip. I tried to turn my attention back to the game, yet my mind was on Daddy's greeting. I was unable to concentrate. After losing a couple of small bets, I packed it in for the afternoon, heading from the casino back to my condo.

As I walked into the condo, I dropped my tote on the table and pulled out my wallet, turning the two cards Daddy had given me over in my grasp. What precisely did he mean would happen when I went to his room around evening time? Most likely he didn't mean for anything sexual to occur. However, the wink he had given me continued kept me guessing, and I figured I should check it out.

I poured a steaming bath and slid in, not sure what I was going to wear and how I was going to act to tempt Daddy. As I

considered his strong body and the firm strength of his hand around mine, I understood that I was getting more excited fantasizing about that hand pushing inside me, pulling my body as I peaked.

While I fantasized, I saw my hand unerringly running down my body, slithering through the water to touch my clit. The warm water of the bath loosened up me, and I began delicately focusing on my stub hovering just beneath the surface. I felt my tension about the late evening easing away, as I lost myself in the joy of the bath.

My fingers were steady, and it wasn't long before I had slipped from my casual state into a forceful one. I tenderly drove my other hand into my pussy, pushing in rhythm with the delicate movement on my clit. As I imagined the filthy things, I hoped Daddy would do to me later, I felt my body tense and I realized I wasn't a long way from peaking.

I slipped a second finger inside myself, moving both of my hands quicker. The sensations were getting difficult to ignore. I pushed my body to the edge before slowing, easing back and appreciating the way my prodding made my body shout at me.

I was unable to sit tight for long, however, and I continued propelling myself until the surge started to spread through my body. As I reclined and delighted in the calming water around me bliss overwhelmed all of my senses. When I started to

unwind once more, I returned into my pussy with three fingers, panting at the pleasant movement.

Pulling my thumb up to brush against my clit, I used my free hand to grab my bosoms. The sensations I was sending through my body were verging on agonizing. However, I felt the need to push ahead to the following climax.

It wasn't far away, and I started to pant as my depleted body went ahead, at last falling into rapture. I hauled my hand out, tenderly rubbing my clit and sliding my entire body into the warm water as I felt the delight expend me.

When I got myself once again into the mood, I washed my hair and got out of the tub. Drying myself with a cushioned purple towel, I took a look in the mirror and smiled, thinking about what sort of trouble I would get into that night.

Standing before my open wardrobe, I flipped through the garments, attempting to discover an outfit that was hot yet not over-the-top. I chose a short dark dress with an open back, calculating that I could go out and stop people in their tracks at a club if it didn't work out with Daddy.

I tried to read a book to relax until my visit. Yet nothing could keep my mind off Daddy's body and the longing I could scarcely contain. One way or another, I figured out how to keep myself busy until the time had come to leave.

Dropping off my vehicle with the hotel's valet service, I got a look at myself in the lift's mirrors. Trying not to grin at how charming I looked, I bombed miserably. Fortunately, no one else was in the lift with me. I got out on Daddy's floor without being humiliated.

I stood before his door, looking down at the room key; not knowing what to do. Would it be ok for me to simply stroll in? Would it be better for me to knock? As much as it would be fun to kick in the door, and give myself wholeheartedly to him, I pick the path of least resistance.

I knocked softly and heard his thick voice from inside. "Come in!" Well, that is it, I guessed. I slid the card through space and opened the door, venturing into his room. It was an ordinary hotel room. I saw Daddy sitting on the bed, wearing a tight dark shirt and pants.

"Hello, darling. Take a load off." I grinned, shutting the door behind me. I strolled over to sit by him on the bed. He set his hand softly on my thigh and I could feel the excitement begin to crawl through me. He gently brushed his fingers down my leg. I contemplated pulling my dress away. He pulled his hand away and stood up.

"Along these lines, like I said before. What about a round of poker?" I nodded. I was eager to do almost anything with Daddy. He sat both of us down at a little table and pulled out a

deck of cards. "Did you bring any chips?" He was smiling, and I shook my head. "Well, it seems that you brought some adorable clothes. Why don't we wager those?"

I paused for a minute to consider his suggestion. At last it clicked. I took a deep breath and answered. "You want to play strip poker, Daddy? I've never played before." He kept on clarifying. His comforting grin quieted my nerves.

"It's really straightforward. Rather than wagering cash, we wager garments. What's more, when we're out of garments we bet...other things." He winked, and I nodded. He dealt out the cards and I looked at mine: another two Aces. My luck was sure great around Daddy.

"Hold up a moment, Daddy. I've just got one garment on."

His smile widened. "Sounds like you'd better not lose."

I shook my head, chuckling to myself as I put it all out there. "I'm all in." I gave him the protected Chelsea gaze intently at, challenging him to call my wager.

"I'll call." Well, that's t what I'd hoped for. He flipped over his cards to uncover a couple of Kings. It was a strong hand that could easily beat me if he's lucky.

He dealt out more cards. I held my breath, holding it until the last card had been dealt. I got another Ace, winning me the hand.

He smiled timidly, pulling his shirt up over his head and tossing it to the side. It hit the edge of the bed, gradually sliding down to the floor. I took the time to gaze at his uncovered chest. I wasn't disappointed. He wasn't buff, yet he had clearly not held back on going to the gym as he got older. There was a slight sprinkling of silver hair on his chest that just made him more appealing.

Daddy picked up and shuffled the cards for the next hand. "Good luck, kid." I stuck my tongue out, coaxing him as he dealt out our cards. I was in the zone, playing some great poker as Daddy lost garment after garment. At last, he lost the last hand and stood up, bumping me as he pulled off his dark boxers.

He seemed to change his mind, pulling them back up and strolling toward me. "Why not help me with these, darling?" I considered yanking them off and pushing him down onto the bed, yet I chose to keep prodding him.

"Hold on, Daddy. Are you unable to strip on your own?" I smiled, totally adoring the feeling of having Daddy precisely where I needed him after such a long time.

He murmured snidely, laughing as he pulled his last piece of clothing off; standing exposed in the hotel room, welcoming me to examine him.

My eyes met his, then my gaze trailed down his neck to get another look at his built chest. His abs were unpretentious but evident, yet they could only hold my attention for so long. At last, I found what would be the principle course for the night.

Daddy's cock was thick and welcoming, even in its casual state. I dropped to my hands and knees and started to creep toward him, checking to see whether I could turn Daddy on.

The view was likely stunning for him. My bosoms hung down into my dress, giving him an eyeful of cleavage as I crept. When I arrived at his feet, I ran a hand delicately up his calf, prodding him by flicking my tongue here and there on his thighs, being careful to stay away from really contacting any of his erogenous zones.

When he was totally excited, I flicked my tongue over his cockhead, grinning at the way in which his body jumped. I kept on prodding him, tenderly blowing my hot breath onto the head of his wet cock, pushing him to the edge until I felt like neither of us could take any more.

I lifted my hand to hold his balls, delicately kneading them as I made moderate, wide circles on his head with my tongue. Daddy

groaned, and I gradually moved my tongue down onto his cock, maneuvering it into my mouth.

Taking as much of it in as possible, I, at last, took his whole length, licking all over as it went totally inside me and was pushed around by my lips and tongue. When I at felt like neither of us could take any all the more, I moved away quickly before plunging back onto his cock, sucking and licking it excitedly.

My hands stroked here and there, crushing and pulling his cock. He fell back on the bed when I pushed him energetically.

I slithered alluringly up his body, cherishing the way in which his eyes devoured my chest. I laid on all fours above him, gradually bringing my mouth down to touch his neck. He tilted his head back as I tenderly sunk my teeth in, delicately bringing my mouth shut and sending a shudder down Daddy's back.

My tongue kept on running down his body, raking over his chest and flicking his areolas. Indeed, even with my eyes shut, I could see Daddy squirming underneath me, frantic for my mouth to return to his cock.

As things were warming up, I teased him again by moving off to the side and snuggling my head to his chest. "Goodnight, Daddy." I pulled a cover over us and faked sleep. However, Daddy wasn't having it. He took my hands and pulled me up to a

sitting position, yanking the ties of my dress from my shoulders and letting them tumble to my sides.

His firm hands kept on stripping me as I sat in the bed, lifting me to pull my dress off. As I sat completely bare, I welcomed Daddy's investigation of my body, feeling the desire that we had denied ourselves for such a long time. His solid hands took me by the shoulders and pushed me down. His hands ran down my body, squeezing my bosoms and solidly testing my sanity.

He kicked the cover from the bed, sliding down to the foot and putting his body between my legs. I shut my eyes and sank into the mattress as his tongue prodded my thighs. His lips snacked tenderly at the zone around my pussy, giving me joy from the firm tip of his tongue.

Daddy squeezed his hands solidly into my knees, pushing them apart as he ran his tongue in a delicate way around my external lips. The desire kept going through my body, yearning for Daddy to satisfy me. But, he was keeping me on the edge, tormenting me with the light brush of his tongue.

When I was unable to take it any longer and propelled myself lower on the bed, squeezing my body into him. He didn't step back. At long last, his tongue met my engorged clit. I let out an edgy groan, and he started to push me quicker and quicker. I felt like I had been prodded for a considerable length of time, waiting for this minute to come.

His lips and tongue didn't give me a moment to unwind, tenaciously exciting my clit and pushing my body to peak for him. He slipped a finger inside, delicately stroking upward and toward him. The delight was felt through me from both inside and outside my body, and I didn't have the foggiest idea how much longer I could last.

When Daddy pushed a second finger inside me, I, at last, felt that my body was his to order and I let go of any control I was attempting to keep. I loosened completely, and was rewarded with another of Daddy's fingers inside me. The pressure of him moving in and out while his tongue moved over my clit was a lot to take, and my body at last detonated into joy.

What I remember most about my first climax with Daddy was the determined beating of my heart as all the muscles in my body strained before unwinding and loading up with unadulterated joy. He eased back his pace altogether, despite everything driving warm joy into me yet unwinding and backing off on my delicate body.

His warm hands lose and afterward accelerated once more, crushing another climax from my worn-out body. As I, at last, fell back against the cushions, I felt Daddy slither up next to me on the bed, putting his hand on my chest and feeling my beating heart.

"All set to rest now, darling?"

"Don't even think about it, Daddy." I pushed him down onto the bed and swung a leg over, straddling his chest between my knees. Delicately descending on his body, I ran my fingernails down his chest and watched the imprints I left. Squeezing my hands down on his chest, I continued down his body, lifting my hips to drift over his erect cock.

I pushed one of my hands into his chest watching as he squirmed and grinned at the agony of my fingernails. I took my other hand and moved it underneath me, delicately placing his cock inside me.

I let out a magnificent groan as I gradually slid down and let in Daddy's cock to move deeply inside me. When I stopped, I looked into his eyes and saw that he was as excited as I, feeling the energy between us.

I lifted myself up and slammed down on his cock, loving the feeling of him pushing inside me. Leaning forward, I dropped my head to meet Daddy's, pushing my tongue into his mouth. He pushed once again into me, and I placed my hands on his head to pull him closer.

While we kissed, I moved my hips forward and back, rubbing Daddy's cock against the walls inside me. His hands pulled me closer. I shut my eyes again and felt his teeth tenderly gnawing my ear. The sensations that shot through me left me too weak to

oppose Daddy's desire, and I turned over onto my back, welcoming him to have his way with me.

He stood, pulling me by the legs down to the foot of the bed. His solid hands took a firm hold on my hips and pushed, entering me once more. My hands lay free at my sides, bobbing as Daddy fucked me, propelling himself inside me over and over.

As he increased the pace, I felt his finger on my clit and my body asked to come once again. Daddy leaned over me as he continued pushing in and out, and I easily recognized that his body just about ready to peak.

His lips met mine once more for a last, profound kiss as we peaked together. I felt my body crushing his cock as he came deep inside me. His lips and tongue were hot and forceful, on my mouth as we came.

I gave a valiant effort to relax as the joy washed over us and the world vanished. At that moment, both of us were as one, and it was euphoria.

When we were done, he lay on me and turned over, pulling me to lie on his shoulder. Our hearts beat together. I stayed until morning. I arose to discover another of his business cards on the table, with a red circle around the telephone number and a heart drawn beneath it.

Sex Story 6: Carnal Love

With a deep inhale of a Sobranie cigarette, Leanne's almond-shaped blue eyes glanced down at the fashion magazine lying open on her lap. Andrew's tongue quickly flicked all over her vagina, while she absentmindedly turned the pages of the magazine, and exhaled out a long tight stream of smoke.

Wisps of smoke hung over her. The smell of tobacco filled the room, radiating from her yellow sundress, which was hiked up high over her midriff to give Andrew the easiest access to her gorgeous pussy. Her long sexy legs hung over the stuffed arms of the armchair, leaving her spread-eagled. Leanne's long blond hair fell over her shoulders, covering her ample, succulent bosoms. She looked gorgeous, fascinating, ravishing, and sexy as hell.

Andrew started to flick and swirl his servile tongue more enthusiastically in order to please his Goddess. He was trying desperately to earn his reward. Andrew worked harder to satisfy her. She completely ignored her slave, taking another long drag, as his tongue immediately fanned her clitoris. Rather than groaning or gazing down at her slave, she blew a series of little round smoke rings over his head, as though he wasn't there. She took two successive mouth hollowing hard drags from her cigarette, held the smoke in her lungs, tilted her head, and blew

a long white thin stream straight up. "Oh, that must be eternal bliss," Andrew wondered inwardly. Regardless of her languid attitude, her stomach started contracting, indicating she was on the brink of an orgasm.

This cat and mouse game had evolved over the past few months when Andrew would fly to Miami from San Francisco to meet with his Queen, Leanne, starting before they were married.

It had evolved from their remarkable qualities and twisted wants. Over the past few months, Andrew had developed a smoking fetish and was more submissive to please his Goddess than ever before, which was perfectly blended with masochistic tendencies. Leanne had become more dominant, with an overpowering sadistic streak. She'd become a heavy smoker.

That night, Leanne devised a wicked plan to fulfill her perverted fantasies in a way that would blend in perfectly with her slave Andrew's as well. She preferred to stay detached unmindful of his wants, smoking, and reading, while Andrew went down on her, putting forth a valiant effort to make her cum.

Leanne had gotten quite good at controlling herself during these sessions. If not for the way that her slave's head was buried in between her thighs, anybody watching would have thought she was bored, amusing herself by looking at a magazine, while she smoked a cigarette. Andrew, fiercely groaned, licked and sucked her pussy.

Occasionally, she looked down at him. When she did, she never acknowledged his strenuous attempts to make her orgasm. If he had done an especially extraordinary job, she would give him the slightest of grins. Those gossamer smiles encouraged Andrew to eagerly and passionately continue his job.

This morning, as she orgasmed, Andrew enthusiastically devoured her juices. Whenever stimulated adequately, Leanne had amazingly wet climaxes. She could squirt such a voluminous amount of cum that Andrew always strived hard to swallow it all. This entertained her. As her back arched, she looked down and blew an overwhelming stream of smoke into her slave's face, hoping it would make him gag and choke on her delectable streaming juices.

Since Andrew didn't smoke, he needed to battle the desire to cough, while continuing to lick and devour her cum. This was her third climax and her third cigarette. When she was completely satisfied, she extinguished her cigarette, rose from the armchair in her living room, and strolled to the kitchen. It had become her routine and a necessity of slave training for her not to recognize her slave's presence for the next thirty minutes.

However, this evening was extraordinary. The doorbell rang. In spite of the fact that Leanne was clothed, she commanded him to answer the door. Andrew was dressed as well, but his hands were bound behind his back, solidly secured to his ankles with a

rope. He wrestled to free himself and stand. She chuckled at his futile attempts.

"Silly pet," she teased, strolling over and, with a tug on the rope, released him of his bonds.

Andrew scrambled to free himself and get to the door. He was relieved to find that the courier boy was gone by then, "It would have been so demeaning to be exhibited as a household slave to the rest of the world," he thought. An enormous box sat on their patio. It was heavy, so he dragged it into the room. Leanne commanded him to open it. He cautiously removed the shipping tape and slid the contents onto the floor. She smiled wickedly, as Andrew gasped in horror.

"Is that a fucking machine?" Andrew shivered.

"Smart slave," she said.

Under her watch, Andrew assembled it. It had a huge powerful electric engine, appended to a wheel, which spun. Every rotation of the wheel made a long steel bar move to and fro. The bar and wheel could be adjusted for short, medium, or long strokes. A remote control enabled the owner to control the speed of the bar's strokes. Leanne had Andrew modify the wheel for the shortest strokes.

The last part of the machine was a black dildo. It was huge; almost 12 inches in length, heavy, thick, and made out of solid, hard plastic.

"Are you certain this will fit inside you?" Andrew enquired restlessly, scratching his head.

"Not me," she stated, winking.

Andrew swallowed hard, his lips trembled, he felt his heart pounding like bass drums, "No fucking way!" he stated, jumping up on his feet in sheer shock.

"Yes fucking indeed, and fucking way, and right now," Leanne asserted, in her dominating voice.

Andrew hung his head and reluctantly pulled off his pants and briefs. She withdrew the horrible looking dildo from the bar, took it to the kitchen, sterilized it, and applied a generous amount of lubricant. When she returned, he had moved the heavy machine before the armchair where they played their games.

Andrew was on all four limbs before the seat, with the steel pole lying between his legs. Leanne walked behind him, attached the dildo to the pole, and without a word slid the tip into his rear end. He moaned noisily. She sat in the armchair, putting her feet on his shoulders, and firmly pushed him in backward, impaling

him onto the huge black cock. It settled somewhere deep inside him. Andrew moaned aloud in agony.

He gazed up at her and saw that she was holding the remote control and smiling. She slid the chair near his face and wrapped her delicate, sexy thighs around his head, forcing her cunt into his servile mouth. She lit a cigarette. Andrew had recently started to cherish the sound of her lighter inflaming the cigarette. He started licking and sucking her pussy devotedly.

He felt the dildo move gradually in and out of his ass. She took another cheek hollowing drag and used the remote to increase the speed. His knees buckled, making his mouth and tongue dive further into her pussy. She breathed out a long moderate stream of smoke over her slave's head.

As she leisurely smoked her cigarette, taking long drags, and breathing out slowly, the machine rhythmically and repeatedly pounded his ass hole. When she had completed her first cigarette, Andrew felt his legs were shaking and he was gasping. With each stroke, the dildo moved faster and faster into his rectum. Goosebumps coursed through his skin; he was feeling dizzy from the exceptional pounding. Leanne slid down in the chair, compelling the dildo deeper into him.

She grabbed her magazine and started looking it over. She took another mouth hollowing drag from her half-completed cigarette, titled her head up, and blew a tight stream of smoke

that nearly reached the ceiling. Andrew worked dedicatedly and enthusiastically on her pussy, as the machine constantly dove deeper and deeper into his butt hole.

All of a sudden, Andrew understood that Leanne had assumed total responsibility for their sexual coexistence—to the point that he had become the woman in the relationship. It was her cock fucking him and he needed to take it. He was never again the pitcher, but now the catcher. The last power shift in their D/S relationship hit him like an electric thunderbolt. His manliness had been stripped away with each stroke. He cried and whimpered like a young girl.

Leanne took a double drag and pressed the button on the remote. The machine thundered, as it moved toward its top speed. The strokes were terribly quick to the extent that Andrew couldn't tell whether they were going in or coming out. In spite of her calm poise, he could see that Leanne was truly making the most of his absolute surrender to her.

By her third cigarette, Andrew was depleted and his rear-end agonizingly ached. She turned her head to one side and breathed out a long slim stream of white smoke. With his legs spread, taking her goliath black cock, seeing her breathing out made Andrew orgasm. He had never climaxed this hard in recent times.

Typically, either she would give her slave a hand job, or let him jerk off, while she watched. Yet, this time it happened without Andrew in any way, touching his cock! He squirted sperm everywhere on the floor underneath her seat. Also, tragically, his bowels loosened at the same time, spurting stool onto the floor behind him.

She put out her cigarette and turned off the machine. He was trembling and extremely embarrassed, but caught between the seat and the dildo, which was still firmly held by his rectum.

"Filthy slave, my, my!" Leanne scolded.

Andrew's cheeks turned redder. She moved the armchair backward, at last allowing Andrew to collapse onto the floor, free of the dildo and the remote-controlled fucking machine. When he got up, he was covered in his own shit.

"You look and smell horrible. From now on, you will take an enema before each of our kinky play sessions," she scolded.

Andrew was wearing a short chain joined to a collar around his neck. She grabbed it and pulled him upstairs to the washroom. Andrew cleaned himself off, and then went to the ground floor and cleaned the mess of his shit.

Afterward, Leanne pulled him back upstairs. He was still naked from the shower, with the exception of the collar around his neck.

In the washroom, she had Andrew kneel down on all his four and set his arms between his legs. She bound his legs and wrists together with a spreader bar. With his arms tightly locked between his legs, his ass was pushed high up in the air. Leanne grabbed an enormous red enema pack. She attached an unusual looking nozzle to the hose.

Andrew hadn't had an enema since he was a kid. As Leanne filled the four-quart elastic sack with lukewarm water, his legs trembled. He was in no frame of mind to question his Goddess, as it would just allow her the choice to paddle her slave hard on his ass. She slipped the peculiar nozzle deep into his rear end, which was very sore from the vicious pounding of the fucking machine. Andrew whimpered.

"Oh, you are such an infant. Ladies take it up the ass constantly and they don't cry like you," Leanne scolded.

Andrew felt something inflating within him. When he looked back, he saw that Leanne was siphoning a little elastic bulb. She saw him and smiled wickedly.

"This is a folio-catheter. It will shield you from making another mess," Leanne chuckled.

The developing pressure of the inflated catheter made Andrew moan once more. He tilted his head and saw the full enema pack delicately swaying to and fro on the shower rod, high above him.

He heard a noticeable snap, which was surely the release valve, as he felt the warm water surge down the tubing into his rectum.

It felt quite hot. Andrew squirmed, as it immediately started flooding his intestines. With the sack hung so high, the pressure was enormous, and he started seriously cramping. His arms and legs were trapped. All he could do was plead to Leanne for mercy, which was another big mistake.

"I have had it with your grumbling!" Leanne said.

She forced a huge ball gag into his mouth, tied it firmly with straps behind his head. With his legs spread, arms bound between them, head stuck to the washroom floor, and mouth firmly gagged, he had no real choice except to take the heated water gushing into his bowels. More terrible yet, the swelled nozzle stopped him from evacuating. He attempted to drive it out, yet it didn't move, and not a drop of water got away. Absolutely vulnerable, he slumped down, completely submitting to the enema and his goddess wife.

It seemed like an eternity before Andrew heard the murmuring sound signaling that the sack was empty. His stomach was agonizingly distended, practically contacting the floor. He felt like a nine-month pregnant woman who had swallowed a watermelon. That was what his stomach closely resembled.

"I will have a cigarette, while that soapy water goes through your colon," Leanne said.

Andrew thought to ask for a release, yet only a couple of murmured sounds got away from the ball gag. Leanne strolled over to the bed, sat on the floor beside it, so he could see her. She lit up, and he watched her smoke, as his gut churned. The lathery water was irritating his bowels, making them severely spasm. As he watched her inhaling and exhaling slowly, relishing her Sobranie cigarette, the spasms became ever stronger, racking his whole body.

The spreader bar kept him from curving his back, so Andrew had to endure every spasm, with no hope of relief. The agony started to blur his vision and thoughts. He could simply make out her taking the last drag, letting a wisp of smoke get away from her luscious lips, before sucking it up her nose. The breath out was so strong that it sent smoke five feet across the room in a thin stream. In spite of the fact that Andrew was sweating hard and his stomach was killing him, witnessing Leanne smoke gave him a rock-hard erection. To his sheer dumb luck and utter dismay, she lit another Sobranie.

Leanne had become a skilled smoker and knew many smoking tricks. She breathed in deeply, and then let the smoke drift out of her mouth, before inhaling it back. She blew another perfect

stream across the room. Another profound inhale was followed by a number of smoke rings.

Then when she, at last, completed her second cigarette, she got up, strolled to the washroom and plunked down on the commode. Andrew couldn't see her; however, he heard her chuckle and get up. She reached up and unfastened the enema bag. Andrew heard Leanne peeing into the bag!

"A golden shower for my golden slave," she stated, chuckling.

Her bladder had probably been extremely full, as it took a few minutes to empty it. She hung the bag back up and Andrew felt her warm pee pour into him. It was extremely embarrassing and erotic all at the same time.

Leanne waited for a couple of more minutes, and then released her slave's bondage. However, she made him lie on his back, not allowing him to empty the four quarts and her urine just yet. She squatted over her slave's mouth. Andrew thought she needed cunnilingus desperately, as she removed his ball gag, but she started peeing once more, this time feeding her slave!

"If you spill one drop, you will be very sorry," Leanne teased and chuckled wickedly.

Andrew reluctantly gulped her piss, and it tasted sour, bitter and awful. He gagged a few times attempting to swallow it. He could taste the beers and wines she'd drunk at lunch—Andrew

desperately battled the urge to vomit. To his sheer shock and bewilderment, Leanne had so much pee left! Then when she was finally done with her peeing, she allowed him to expel the enema in the toilet, while she watched her slave. It was mortifying and humiliating beyond expressions.

Unfortunately, it was just the beginning of Andrew's plight, as she forced him to take two additional enemas to wipe out the soap sods. Each time, Leanne restrained him in a similar manner, causing Andrew to hold four quarts for quite a while, as she smoked a couple more cigarettes.

During the second enema, she set nipple clamps on Andrew. This was his first experience in them, and they hurt like hell. However, the third enema was the most unimaginably horrible of the three, as she paddled him the whole time it was gushing into him. Also, to his sheer shock, she paddled hard as if he was a prisoner on a life sentence. She had powerful wrists so she could deliver a swat with all the power it takes for long everlasting red impression, over and over and again and again with the same impeccable intensity. Andrew's ass was brilliant red and burning with an itching sensation when Leanne finally wrapped up.

After completing the last enema, which was thoroughly clean, Andrew could hardly gather the strengths of his numb feet. Leanne yanked the short chain joined to the collar, and pulled

him up, and then led him down the stairs. He nearly fell on his face while in transit to the living room.

Leanne had brought down the spreader bar. She placed it between her devoted slave's legs and tied his hands between them. Andrew was too depleted to beg and so he obliged, never allowing his goddess wife a chance to be infuriated again.

After Leanne slid the dildo back inside Andrew, she placed a comfortable cushion before the armchair and positioned herself so that her slave's servile face was settled in her cunt once more. Andrew's head was bent at an awkward angle. However, he put forth a valiant effort to lick her, please her and satisfy her.

Before long the fucking machine was quickly pumping his rear end, but deeper than the last time. Leanne commented that his licking and sucking was not up to the mark and grabbed her riding crop. As Andrew strove hard to pick up the pace and endeavor to satisfy his Goddess wife, he felt the snap of the crop on his naked ass. It truly stung!

When Leanne turned up the machine and spanked his butt cheeks, it somehow energized Andrew to fulfill her carnal desire. She orgasmed like Niagara Falls and squirted cum right down his throat.

Her back arched with each squirt. For a minute, he wondered if he might suffocate! Spurting and coughing between swallows, he

figured out how to swallow every drop of her precious cum, while giving her pussy the devoted attention it required. She reclined back against the cushion, and lit another cigarette, as the fucking machine continued pounding Andrew mercilessly. Leanne gazed down at him and grinned wickedly.

Although Andrew was extremely depleted, he came hard this time. As each orgasmic spasm shook his body, the spreader bar horrendously prevented him from curving his back. Leanne blew a tight stream of white smoke into his face. She cherished watching him drifting between delight and distress.

"You know why you came so often today? In the last enema, I gave you a double dose of Viagra," Leanne said.

Before Andrew could react, she leaned forward, squeezed his nose, forcing his mouth to open, and her luscious lips crashed onto his parched ones, blowing smoke into his mouth. He coughed and choked. She repeated this procedure a few times. He was coughing so hard he could hardly breathe, while the automated fucking machine kept fucking his butt hole relentlessly.

At long last, she smacked his face hard and stuck her fingers down his throat. Andrew choked, yet didn't struggle. Leanne took one final cheek hollowing drag from her Sobranie and then blew a plume straight up his nose. Andrew gagged and coughed like a baby. She took pride in crafting the devious pleasures.

Leanne kissed him passionately, turned off the machine, and released him of his bondage. Andrew took a shower, cleaned the living room, practically crawled up the stairs and climbed into bed beside her. She cuddled close, putting her mouth beside his ear.

"You did excellent today, slave. I'm going to try the next higher setting tomorrow," Leanne murmured.

Her words terrified and excited Andrew. He shivered and goosebumps coursed through his skin. She straddled him shoving his hard cock into her pussy. He was too depleted to even shake his hips and lay sedately beneath her. She pushed a pillow under his rear end, and rode him like a rodeo cowgirl. Leanne fucked him hard draining the life out of his balls until they both came. Then, she collapsed over him.

"Yes. I've decided to try the next higher setting next time," she murmured in his ear again. Andrew only swallowed hard as his eyes felt too heavy to keep open.

She grabbed his hair and kissed him passionately, driving her tongue into his mouth. He could taste the tobacco on her breath, as their tongue lapped and intertwined.

She instructed her slave to open his mouth wider and spit a few times down his throat. Andrew anxiously gulped her saliva.

She relaxed on top of him. As they drifted off to sleep. Andrew was amazed that the idea of being fucked by his Goddess wife again excited him. Leanne now claimed him inside and out. He felt content and completely fulfilled being her bitch.

Sex Story 7: Birthdays Are for Everyone

"Everyone, settle down" the disk jockey announce and the rowdy hall suddenly fell quiet, "Who's ready to rock with the best DJ in the country?"

The party goers hooted, finding the groove when he worked his turntable to give a scratchy noise.

"Yeah, that's what I thought" he bragged, basking in the new found vibration that was in the room, "Yo. I want the whole room to make some noise for the birthday girl Ariana!"

The crowd hooted again and a frenzy broke out when the disk jockey scratched his turntable again and let the music play. He had brought the groove to the party and everyone started to move their bodies to the music.

"Hey, Nick" someone called in the din and he spun around to find the source. The chubby guy with the familiar face made its way through the crowd with a drink in his hand.

"Hey, Brad" He said putting his hands out for a handshake, the other man clasped his hand with his and shook it, "Damn. The party is too loud"

Brad smiled.

"The DJ has been ass all evening. I think he's trying to redeem himself before the losers leave" he said.

"Hey, man. Calling these people losers is going to hurt some feelings" Nick noted.

Brad shrugged and allowed himself a sip of the drink before he replied.

"You know. You're not a loser so I might just have to warn you. This would be the wildest party you've ever been to" Brad said into his ears.

"What? Why? I went to hotter parties as a five-year-old" Nick hissed.

"You see, Nick. I'll bet you five hundred bucks and you'll see I'm telling the truth" Brad bragged.

"What do you mean, Brad?" Nick quizzed, puzzled by the cryptic comments at the quality of the party even when he could bore himself out by just walking around for a while.

Brad looked around and made sure no one was close enough to hear him then he leaned in and spoke into his ears, drawing his words out for effect.

"Do you have a condom on you?" Brad asked.

Nick sensed the direction it was going to and he smiled.

"Nah. Is there some girl you're trying to fuck, Brad?" He asked, looking around to sniff out the easy work from the bunch.

"I am not trying to fuck any girl, Nick. You ask too many questions. They are trying to fuck us" Brad laughed out hysterically, and sipped on his drink whilst shaking his head to confirm what he had said.

"What does that mean? Who's us? Who's they and why are they trying to fuck us?" He asked in rapid succession.

"I don't think you've observed closely, Nick. But this is THE Ariana Leighton hosting her twenty first birthday. We're going to get laid" he ground out the words, looking around them for eavesdroppers.

"And you know this how? What makes you so sure?" Nick chuckled dismissively.

"The loser would leave, Nick. And the fun would begin. Ariana had planned an orgy for tonight!" Brad wheezed.

Nick had no special way of noting who the losers were at the party but after some time, he noticed a certain section of the party had gone and the hall had started to gain the dull smell of sexual perversion. Everywhere he turned some couple seemed to be making out and the most innocent of those would be rated for

adults if it were to be on screen. He looked for Brad in the room and found him somewhere close by the bar with a bottle of Vodka, talking with a strange girl.

"Brad!" He called as he made his way towards his friend.

Brad smiled eagerly when Nick approached him and with an exaggerated sense of courtesy, he introduced him to the girl he had been speaking with.

"Nick, this ebony queen right here is Trisha. She's a brilliant sophomore and a lady who is not afraid to go down if you know what I mean. Trisha, this is my friend Nick. Not the best of the bunch but a good friend" he said, bowing and gesturing all the while he spoke.

Nick took Trisha's hands and they shook.

"Nice to meet you, Nick" she said.

"Hey, pleasure's all mine. You're friends with Ariana?" Hs asked.

"No. But my friends are. I thought I could join them for a good time" she said, smiling.

"That's nice" Brad imputed before Nick could speak, "I see your friends heading in that direction, Trisha" he said pointing towards a group of girl who followed a small crowd into the corridor that led to the next story of the building.

"Yeah. I think Ariana has a private party or something" she answered, taking the hint and walking away from the Nick and Brad, "see you guys up there?"

Nick nodded.

"Yeah. We'll be there in a moment" Brad said, watching her walk away from them and joining her friends. Neither of the duo said a word to the other until she'd disappeared from sight.

"What the fuck was that, Nick? Brad asked, "Girls like that don't do chivalry. They just want to fuck and forget your face. And you're trying to be nice?"

"What are you talking about, Brad. I hadn't even spoken two sentences" Nick said, draining his glass.

Brad blustered and looked up at the ceiling, as though by some divine revelation he could tell what happened in piecemeal.

"You think they're fucking up there?" Nick asked, naively.

"I'll get condoms for us both. Don't go anywhere" Brad said and walked away from him.

Brad's brows jumped with an *I told you so* definiteness when they were let into the room and they saw naked bodies and semi naked people making out in the room. It was the most lustful orgy Nick had ever seen and he was surprised how Brad had

known before him. Brad was cool on campus because of him. Brad was the side kick.

"Hey, Nick" Ariana was naked too and shameless. The entire room was shameless. She sauntered through the crowd of bodies and walked towards them. "You boys, no clothes in my room"

She pulled on Nick's shirt and indicated he take it off.

"I looked for you all week, Nick. Brad told me you flew ho... Yes, the pants too and your underwear" she pointed out, "there is alcohol everywhere if you boys want to get loose. There are bitches and Nick, if you want ass, I'm here baby" she kissed his naked chest and scurried back to the guy she had been making out with before their arrival.

Brad held Nick's hand and pushed a condom into his open palm.

"Went to parties like these as a five-year-old?" He teased, settling down slowly to the girl who was closest to him.

"Nick, over here" someone called.

It was a sea of bodies. Nick thought he counted over thirty people in the room but more people brought their heads from beneath other people and it was all a vague, messy arithmetic in his mind.

"Trisha" he mouthed the name and like one conjured, he started to make his way towards her.

Trisha and her friends stuck to themselves, caressing their bodies and sticking fingers into themselves.

"How did you see me from such a distance?" He asked, grabbing hold of her outstretched hand and pulling him into the jungle of her friends.

"I've been waiting. So where do we begin? Get your dick sucked?" She winked and like magic he felt lips on his cock, sucking the length of his rod.

Trisha leaned in and kissed him softly, caressing his body. The sloppiness of the fellatio made him heady. He lifted his head to catch an image of the one who gave such good head but Trisha's weight pressed him down. A strange tongue held his ear lobe between wet lips and started to lick it. It was pure paradise, all the senses of his body being engaged at the same time.

"Never fucked a black girl before, have you?" She asked biting his lips and bathing him in her own perspiration. She slid away from him seductively and joined the girl who had given him head so that it made two of them on his cock. Another girl took her place and began kissing him.

Fireworks in his head set off when Trisha deep-throated his cock. She soaked his cock in her saliva and deep-throated again.

Wherever did they find these girls? The voice in his head asked. They knew pleasure and gave it like nothing he'd ever felt.

"Leave the man alone, Megan" Trisha said to the girl who kissed him and held him upright, "Come get this pussy, Nick. Doggy style"

She bent over and spread her neatly shaved ebony juice box for him. It was surreal that all the noise he heard was of fleshy laps tapping against one another and of moaning and grunting. He had slipped into a porn movie and he was trying a role he had barely rehearsed for.

One of Trisha's friends came over and started to kiss him on the lips. The texture of her tongue on his told him which one she was. She was the first to suck his cock. She kissed him and stroked his cock before helping him prime Trisha's pussy. Nick watched the entire sequence play itself out like a baby being taught to pee.

Trisha's pussy welcomed him and she moved her hips back and forth to fuck him before he started to stroke. Her game was good and even her friend whose name he could not ask for giggled at his strokes against hers.

The girl rubbed his bare chest as he fucked Trisha like a wild animal to save face. Trisha was unmoved by the ferocity of his lashing against her pussy even though it was tight enough to make her uncomfortable.

"Hey guys" Brad said, stepping carefully towards them with an erect penis. He had no condom on.

Shit!

He watched his cock plowing in and out of Trisha's tight pussy without a condom on. How had he misplaced it? He thought to stop but that would be such a mood killer. He played the conversation that would most likely ensue in his head.

Hey, Nick. Trisha would ask. *Why'd you stop.*

hm, just one moment while I look for my condom. He would reply

What? A condom? Oh white boy! She would moan and tell him off.

It would be so embarrassing. Fucking her and making her moan like the rest of the room was not embarrassing and he knew what side he would rather be on. He withdrew from her and Trisha laid him on his back. Trisha's skillful friend engaged Brad and the rest of the gang mingled with the crowd.

"Where's your fucking condom, Brad?" He whispered when Brad was close enough.

"I have no idea" Brad answered and looked to Nick's cock, found it bare and shot a questioning look.

"This room has to be a condom repellant. I can't find mine too" Nick murmured.

"I see you guys never stop talking to each other like you're in love" Trisha remarked.

"Ah, there you are" Ariana popped her head between both girls who sucked on Nick and Brad's dick. "I wanted to ask you first before someone popped it. I'm trying to get my ass fucked tonight, Nick"

She took a swig of the bottle she carried and blubbered as harsh alcohol made its way down her throat.

"Hey, I'd like to see" Trisha said and turned around to see it was Ariana. She acted surprised and somewhat star struck, Nick noted. Trisha was a fan girl and it was hilarious to watch.

"I'm going to need some of that" Nick requested and sat up to take a gulp of it.

Ariana's ass was tight and they lubed it for several minutes before Nick could go all in. Even when he did, it was uncomfortable since she accepted all of his cock in her ass hole. The slobbering oil lube made the affair slippery and more intense. His body jerked with the motions as he fucked her ass and she cried out with pain and pleasure.

"All that fucking cock in my ass!" She cried, ordering him to fuck her harder. She was going to be so sore the next morning, having her ass popped for the first time by an amateur like himself but Nick knew he had to make it worthwhile.

He clashed against her cheeks relentlessly, digging deep into her tight ass until the only border between them both was their skin.

"You want to try mine?" Trisha asked, sneaking from behind and stroking his ear lobes with her tongue. She held him from behind like a lover and kissed his neck as though he were not cock deep in another girl's ass. The temptation that Trisha posed was one that he could not deny.

She had taken possession of him in one night and he knew she would be something he would have to keep for a longer time. He slipped out of Ariana's ass and Ariana rolled to the floor, sprawling herself out like cement plastered atop the hard ground.

"Try mine" Trisha whispered into his ears and it was enough to turn him to her.

They lay on the floor, facing each other and forgetting the entire room in their one moment of copulation that was detached from their social environment. They cuddled each other like lovers.

She placed her legs over his waist and he slipped beneath her to insert his cock into her ass. It was just as tight as Ariana's but her fleshy booty made it more sensuous.

He gasped and she moaned, each exploring the depths and lengths of their sexual means. Slowly and softly, they brought each other to orgasm. He filled her and she felt him.

It was something otherworldly, a work of art, order in the midst of such chaos that two people would find a way to make love when everyone else was focused on fucking. That he was fucking her ass so pleasantly was the beginning of the ecstasy, it was how he held her, to himself, unwilling to share, showing possession that made her cum for him.

He came for her, in her tight asshole, losing himself to the rhythm of his motions. If an artist had been there to document the feeling they offered each other, he would have started a new religion.

They kissed as they both came, Trisha from her ass and him from his member without missing a beat. Indeed, there was nothing more beautiful than a man and woman, without the barrier of intentions, making love so peacefully.

CPSIA information can be obtained
at www.ICGtesting.com
Printed in the USA
LVHW050433100221
678895LV00006B/1035

9 781914 107412